Curiosity Killed the Sphinx

and Other Stories

Curiosity Killed the Sphinx

and Other Stories

Katherine L. Holmes

Hollywood Books International
Hollywood, California

Published by Hollywood Books International
an Imprint of Press Americana
The Press of Americana:
The Institute for the Study of American Popular Culture
7095-1240 Hollywood Boulevard
Hollywood, California 90028

http://www.americanpopularculture.com

This book is a work of fiction, a product of the author's imagination. Any relation to actual character, place, incident, or any other matter is purely coincidental.

Cover photo: Split Rock Lighthouse by A. E. Crane

Holmes, Katherine L.
Curiosity killed the Sphinx and other stories / Katherine L. Holmes.
p. cm.
ISBN 978-0-9829558-3-3
I. Title.
PS3608.O4943545C87 2012
813'.6--dc23
2012006556

TABLE OF CONTENTS

CURIOSITY KILLED THE SPHINX

The week's shipment of cheese not having come to the Co-op, Jill crosses to the university farm campus. She turns from the buildings where she has nutrition classes. The air in them is as stale as a barn before spring.

Along the raw landscaped terraces, she guesses at the tumult of branches, whether they are spirea or lilac or viburnum. At a crab apple tree, she notices the drastic swerves of the limbs.

She's reminded of Glenn demonstrating how computer passwords lead to stored data. Lost files were like fallen leaves. She was choosing a name for her own files in the computer at the university hospital. That benefit didn't amount to a twig, not even a bud, in the computer system there.

Glenn brought a present to the laboratory operator's room after Jill began working at the hospital. Windowless and L-shaped, the room contained little to distract the operators from reading off lab results on the telephone. It was 1981 but most of the doctors didn't know how to operate the computers that were slowly being installed at the nurses' stations.

On the shelf above Jill, Glenn displayed odd, lumpy looking objects, decorative like dwarf hats. He brought them in a box that was usually used for print-outs.

"They're bigger than crab apples and smaller than eating apples." Jill was dubious.

"Experiments from the farm campus," Glenn explained to Becky, the other lab operator on duty.

Having seniority, Becky felt she should receive the apples somehow. "Do they have something to do with Apple computers?" she wondered. But then she was nodding over the phone, saying "Thanks for holding" as she pulled up a patient's liver labs.

"Glenn, what's the formula for skipping down to my footnote page?"

The dwarf apples meant that Glenn had been reading her paper on apples in the computer. He had done that when he was maintaining the gargantuan mainframe system. Amid subterranean passageways, his working area was wintry with terminals and hardware that resembled refrigerators and freezers.

"It's called a command. Here, it's in the index of the editing program." He brushed her contours behind Becky's back.

In her first month as lab operator, Jill found out that Glenn was as admired as a doctor, despite his jeans and his T-shirts. He was simply square and bronze, his brown T-shirt setting off his hazel eyes, unusual with his sandy hair. His eyes had a metallic glint when he was pleased at work. Jill didn't know if it was the lighting or the atmosphere. The woman who hired them both, Ursula, had gray eyes that could turn silver.

Glenn tapped another box and said in his quiet tone, "Print-outs too."

When he was gone, Jill said, "I'd like to figure out the password to Glenn's files."

"Probably no one can," Becky replied. "Glenn doesn't often bring presents to our bleak office." She mused at the blobs on the shelf. In the mazy old hospital, newspaper blurbs about out-of-the-ordinary treatments were usually the celebration balloons.

"Glenn must have been reading my paper on apples," Jill hinted, preparing to tell Becky about their relationship. She stared at the page in her computer, the fortified baby food recipe with apples and ground nuts.

"You'd have an easier time getting into a vault than into Glenn's files," Becky said. "He's our wizard."

"He found out my password."

When the computer crawled or crashed and the whole hospital was put on hold, Glenn gave the dependable prognosis.

A ringing telephone kept Becky from answering. Another button began blinking at Jill, then another.

"The rush before doctor rounds," Becky declared. She was hesitant where men other than her husband were concerned. When she joked about doctors that would deluge their office if it wasn't unmarked, her gums showed their pink scallops. But her eyes were sympathetic and she was continually appreciative of her marriage.

A sloping sidewalk takes Jill towards the dark mattresses of the fields. She walks, breathing in the fresh air of this open space. It will smell of fertilizer in a few weeks. Since she came to the city, she's had energy lows during the dregs of winter. She's theorized that nutritional deficiencies are exacerbated by city life. Now they know about AIDS at the hospital and even though she doesn't see how she could possibly have the disease incubating, she is as obsessed with a cold as the people there are.

A student from an agrarian county is the typical student on the farm campus. Jill used to complain to Glenn that every errand in the city required added steps, deft timing, and stony standing. By the end of February, Jill felt fatigued, not exercised. In the snowbanks of the mainframe computer, Glenn was as active as a lifeguard. He had suggested another factor then. She wasn't used to her REM sleep being ruined by both a man and her schedule. Skeptically, he watched her convolutions into graduate school.

This year, the city sprawls like a huge hospital. Since it is disaster-ridden, procedure is required. The pedestrians go through pale tunnels; the cars are often crippled to wheelchair speed. Because she's a student, Jill feels like a species of fungi. She's not supposed to lament the loss of a man who gave her bite-sized apples as a present. That was when the trouble started.

At the hospital, the devoted females were alert to any symptoms of infatuation since many had suffered it. Even Jean, reliably lumbering into their office for the morning print-outs and the gossip.

"Look at those apples," she said. "They look specially ordered for pediatrics."

"Glenn brought them," Jill replied.

"They're not crabs," Jean determined, picking up an apple and rotating it. "As if a glimpse of Glenn isn't enough of a day-brightener."

"They're hybrids."

Jean looked at each of the other apples, smiling.

"He brought them for Jill," Becky said as helpfully as if she was touting a lab result.

Jean was visibly balked. She wasn't prepared for her favorite to settle on a particular female. She gave a shrug, the sign of the hospital, and took the print-outs that came from the subterranean computer.

Between doctor rounds, Ralph, the recently-hired department head, dropped in. He had to show his disdain for the work-study that Ursula organized. Jill had a microbiology book cracked and Becky was working on a house insurance form. Ursula gave them relief from the incessant calls that took up a third of the day, having worked with the computer system since it was no larger than an incubator. She left the labs to foster it. In Ursula's brain was the most historically complete index of the present computer system. She had recently been disinterred from the mainframe office to join the programmers on the mezzanine floor.

Ralph often called her to come down and see him. Even the male employees were dismayed at Ralph overseeing Ursula.

"Busy morning, girls?" he needled them.

Jill looked at how his suit jutted at his sloping shoulders. A heavy notebook seemed to burden him. If it were open, he would show photographs of computer equipment as if he were showing new car models. His thinning black hair erupted from a combing that could only be ahead of its time.

"Girls, keep track of the print-outs that obstetrics requests. We've got a terminal up there now and Ursula's had a session with the nurses. I hope we can phase out this lab operator job in a year."

This was Ralph's warning since he had come.

Standing near Jill, Ralph wheedled, "What are these? Your lunch? Five funny apples?"

"Glenn gave them to me. They're maggot-free."

Ever since her private conference with Ralph, Jill understood how he could retrieve hatred out of nice men. She had seen one of Glenn's co-workers shout four-character computer codes at him.

Alone with Jill, Ralph went over the hospital map for print-out delivery. In order to discuss the instructions for critical wards and the locked psychiatric ward, Jill had to sit near Ralph. He said he would answer her every question.

But he was scrutinizing her clothing the way he did when she clattered into the computer room downstairs.

"Is there something wrong with jeans or shoes?" Jill asked. "I am a student, you know."

"The nurses on the floor should recognize you by now. But you must always wear stockings." Then he proved that she was wearing nylons with the toe of his shoe.

Ralph examined the apple presents while Jill, under his sleeve, flipped through the pages of a transplant patient's labs. He was often reduced to asking Glenn for help with the enormous computer. Glenn and the other men who worked with it were stingy with Ursula's passwords.

Upstairs, Ralph was full of admonishments. "Girls, you don't always remember. List the station print-outs before the research print-outs." The metal door latched shut.

Becky was leaving too, for an afternoon appointment. She giggled, "Have you heard Glenn worrying that he could turn into a Ralph?"

"It's becoming a lament, isn't it?" Jill replied.

Even Ursula was drawn to the bright blood-colored apples when she came to verify that Yi Wu was covering for Becky. She smiled benevolently at Jill finishing a phone call and Yi Wu filling out papers in Chinese.

"They'll have to get all the apples down from the trees, I guess." Ursula was enigmatic, even about the weather.

"Glenn brought the apples," Yi Wu imparted.

"They keep the teeth clean after lunch." Although the shimmer of Ursula's gray hair and eyes had a maternal power about it, her workspace resembled both a kitchen and a spaceship. It was the female power of the mother-in-law, Jill felt, that made her jittery around Ursula. That or Ursula'a high intelligence. Glenn might have gotten his mysterious sphinx smiles from her. Ursula's secrets might as well have been stashed in a bottle that hovered near the moon.

Jill answered her with information. "Apples that size might be the best thing for lunch boxes. There's more peel to them, more vitamins."

"Happy apples." Ursula's eyes went silver like the silver strands in her hair.

In the afternoon, Zanny appeared. At the shift change, she delivered print-outs and exchanged personal data with the orderlies and nurses. Zanny was irrepressible, not having learned either the computers or the tongue-in-cheek ways of their department.

"What are these? Little red apples?"

"They're experiments," Jill answered. Becky had prepped her on Denise, known as Zanny. Paradoxically, the domestic Becky got a start from Zanny's candid, often crass remarks. Glenn avoided her when he could. Yi Wu inscrutably grinned at another American novelty.

"What will they experiment on here next?" Zanny's pendulous earrings and swaying umber-colored hair completed her extrovert exclaims. Sometimes when she gulped for air, her tongue made a lizard leap to her lip.

Yi Wu said, "Did you know the smaller apples are more nutritious because they have more vitamins?"

"How?" Zanny looked from Yi Wu to Jill. "Are you experimenting with apples?"

"Smaller apples have more peel to the volume," Jill explained.

"Who's experimenting with apples?" Zanny persisted.

"A friend of Glenn's," Yi Wu said.

"So that hunk is distributing apples like Johnny Appleseed?"

"They're for me," Jill resorted to telling her. "Because of my paper."

"Isn't he weird, that wet blanket? Do you know Glenn very well? I didn't think anyone could. Look, this apple's an egghead! Do they taste like anything?" Zanny was too spontaneous to dislike and she was often aghast.

"I don't know," Jill said.

"Taste one."

"You taste one."

"What if their experiment failed?"

They all shrieked because Jill didn't want to try an apple experiment either.

The air near the practice farm acres is bracing. Jill's city claustrophobia is chronic in the winter. Snowdrifts and ice complemented the glass and concrete buildings. Inside was outside. Somewhere in this, she lost Glenn. Today is the first time her feet haven't been on a gleaming concourse since she walked with Glenn along the Mississippi. The river road rounded the older neighborhood between the university and the downtown. Glenn's command, "Don't go around with Zanny" seemed like a rigid program then.

Jill protested, "There are Zanny's in small towns. She gave a bum a blanket because he was sleeping in a freeway cave."

Zanny's joking about a lab technician bringing her rubber gloves on her white mouse date wasn't a punch line. But Jill's hometown friend, the one who was a scream, presented her with a colossal cookie shaped like a man's package and clothed only in sugar. Afterwards the baker burnt a guy at a party and went to mass in the morning.

Jill took a walk around Lake of the Isles with Zanny the Saturday before. Zanny's uptown apartment wasn't far from Jill's.

Zanny exclaimed, "So there *is* something behind the computer man's mystique. Glenn was a perfect poker face when you filled the lab operator opening. I had no idea you knew him."

Finally, Jill was telling another woman how Glenn was perfect. He was so perfect that he was a strain, too kind about her flaws. They met in a microbiology lab and no, Jill found herself saying, he wasn't a procedure at night.

"And to think that when you're apart, he's only unfaithful with a computer. It's hard to hang onto men around here."

When Jill loitered near an opulent home fronting the lake, a man recognized Zanny with a smile. That was the second on their walk. In a waist-length jean jacket, Zanny's shape was old-fashioned but still successful. And she was girlish, not filling out the jacket. Usually, Jill received stray glances. Her straight shoulder-length black hair and bangs gave her an Egyptian prettiness.

Jill consoled Zanny. "I had a few disappointments before Glenn."

"I've had dozens of disappointments. Talking about experiments. Out of so many men, you'd think something would last."

"You're kidding." Jill scrutinized the face of the approaching jogger.

"I had an awful childhood," Zanny said matter-of-factly. Taking psychology courses was her off-hours hobby though she couldn't sit down long enough to get a degree.

Since Jill hadn't known exactly who Zanny was, Glenn won that round of a game the computer enthusiasts played. "I Know Something You Don't Know" preoccupied them after a premature November blizzard. The game started after Ralph began surveillance of their computer games.

RULES: Programs can be modified while getting around the system. Ralph has programmed a command to forbid the playing of computer games except when he designates. The wizard operates as a human being, not a robot, getting his way while getting around the rules.

OBJECT: To know about more files than the next player. Jill considers this if she puts information about Zanny in her file. Zanny's childhood, her haphazard eating habits, her dependence on Coca-Cola or Doctor Pepper or Royal Crown Cola or Shasta Cola.

POINTS: The amount of access a player has. For example, Ursula was initially the only person who could access secret files containing all the phone numbers where doctors could be reached in emergencies.

SKILL & CHANCE: The skilled computer operator can keep a file inviolable in the system. This is a magic art to the women in the lab operator's office. The reason for that goes back to Becky. She entered a program she didn't understand and lost files of information, what she confessed was a $10,000 mistake. Secret identities, private passwords, and hidden files increase the element of chance. The formidable player, Glenn, somehow gets past the password padlocks.

PLAYERS: The term user, coined in Ralph's generation, grates on the younger players. They strive for an ethical alternative to obedience and the command pyramid. Never making Becky's $10,000 mistake, they want to prove that Ralph uses Ursula to gain money and status.

TO START: In the first round, Ralph hid a file that set up the computer games in the system. He has added a clock mechanism that records the time and identity of game users. If the players find the file, they can switch off the new program. Then they can play a real computer game without leaving a trace.

When Jill descended into the labyrinth labeled with hospital hieroglyphics, she passed through doors with combination doorknobs. Beyond was the computer area, humming and frosty as the snowy boulevards outside.

The starting point of "I Know Something You Don't Know" was Ralph. He didn't turn to Jill; he spoke in profile like an Egyptian picture in a pyramid chamber.

"That laboratory log needs to be Xeroxed," he gestured.

Since Ralph was still dependent on Ursula, she was in the sealed room, gesturing at print-outs. She might turn her head from the computer terminal, her eyes silver here. "Fun, fun, fun," she often said when she showed anyone a computer shortcut, her strange eyes childlike.

The white panels were igloo-like and, to Jill, the codes on the computer screens might be on wizard hats. Glenn also gleamed there. And because he and Jill had a secret that couldn't be transmitted through the wires under the flooring panels.

But Jill was trying to find out something for herself — why her schedule was often opposite Glenn's. This had been going on since the early November blizzard. Lately, he was usually working the shift or weekend that she had off.

They had a spat after Christmas. Jill thought that was part of their relationship but it brought a whole evening down. She wanted to go for a breather at Como Park greenhouse, a vague attempt at an anniversary. He wanted to go cross-country skiing. Still, he was annoyed in the car, not having time to go anywhere but the university golf course.

Pulling into another of the metropolis' predictable playgrounds, Glenn asked, "Are you still hanging around with Zanny on the sly?"

"I never hung around with her. She's lonely. We mostly talk at work. Well, sometimes we go to the Sixes and Sevens bar."

They were both nettled. The snow at the golf course was pounded to the sheen of hospital linoleum.

"I'll bet she's a mindbender a minute."

"At least she's a person who can admit what's going on with her. What do you have to hide? You're all intrigue and intensity. Technology. So much secretiveness."

"I said, don't discuss me around Zanny," Glenn said, getting out of his Datsun to unstrap the skis.

Jill had to question whether she would be content in such a day-to-day landscape. Glenn's emotional thermostat was almost always set on cool.

They had the homemade pizza Glenn loved that night, made with whole grain crust and three cheeses from the Co-op: cheddar, mozzarella, and parmesan.

"What did you do with those hybrid apples?" Glenn wondered at her apartment. "To think I actually ate your baby food formulas."

"I tried one and gave the others to the birds. After the early blizzard."

Glenn had to work the night shift at 11:00 p.m.

Happening like a computer crash, a severe one that requires an outside expert, the round of "I Know Something You Don't Know" abruptly ended. On a Sunday in January, Jill was on duty in the laboratory operator's room. Glenn was scheduled to start his shift when she was leaving, at three in the afternoon.

Jill hadn't seen Glenn for a week although he stayed at her parents' during Christmas break. He was unusually enthusiastic to spend time in rural bars with dartboards. Despite that, her mother was enthusiastic about him. When her mother had an opportunity to introduce Glenn, she groped for another term besides *boyfriend*.

Jill wasn't so quick to call Glenn perfect now. She predicted that he wouldn't even stop by her office before his shift. At her terminal, she listed a print-out of her own fortified, affordable baby food, to be picked up downstairs.

The metal door clicked and Jill jumped. Lately, she felt the way she did when a doctor called and asked for lab results in a leisurely voice, then backtracked and skipped around for results that lead up over many pages to the word *expired*.

Even though Glenn entered the bare room like a shaft of light, Jill felt reduced. She comprehended why so many nun-like women worked in medical areas.

He stood at her computer, reading her paper. "Do you want to set up a table for those figures?"

"No. I don't care," Jill said. "Have you read this?"

His broad smile hid his liabilities. His knowing something she didn't know, if he was still in love with her, was unnerving. She groped for his arm and cupped his elbow in her hand until he could feel the cold metal of her bangles.

Glenn kissed her and said, "I've got to get down to the computer."

"My mother called again. I've been wondering if she should keep referring to you as my boyfriend."

Glenn just teased. "I was looking for your high school boyfriend. I thought I heard her say something about him. Come downstairs after you're done?"

"I've got a print-out to pick up."

Jill shivered into the core of corridors where she imagined mummies were hidden. This was hardly the place to regain closeness with Glenn.

Glenn didn't even look up. "I've got to concentrate to get these game controls switched back. I think I found another ID for Ralph in here."

It was hardly the place, even to snack on the brownies she brought.

"This system is like a Swiss bank. Files stashed everywhere."

Absorbed with his partially-solved brainteaser, Glenn flipped from a page that looked like hieroglyphics to one that might be Cantonese or Greek. Such screens gave Jill a pang of panic.

"Write down these combinations while I try them. M-E-M-$-3-R, M-E-N-$-3-R, M-E-S-$-3-R, M-E-T-$-3-R. Wow."

Jill began to wonder if anywhere would be the place.

"Stored correspondence. Ralph's got a computer friend in Chicago. Look at this."

Ursula had recently hooked up their university hospital with the county hospital and Chicago hospitals.

"Put off by a young guy who must have developed his pectoral muscles shoveling in the sticks because he couldn't work out his height." Glenn looked at Jill now. "His friend knows the type."

Jill had to laugh.

"You're in this one. Updates to personnel. Tentative layoff date, one year. Becky might get promoted. Look at what he wrote here. As if he knows more about it than Ursula. I'm her protégé, her wizard!"

"Do you want my brownies instead of a cafeteria bismark?" Jill interrupted.

"He's recommending that computer room personnel take psychological tests! He thinks Larry's too volatile. Doesn't know him."

"Glenn, I'm not enjoying this."

"Yeah. That's the intelligence too. You're not enjoying things." When Glenn turned towards her, his eyes had the eeriness of Ursula's. "You're going to deliver print-outs every day as the computers get installed. Maybe it's for the better. And Ralph wants me on a standard hospital schedule, nights. That should solve your difficulties."

"What do you mean? I never see you as it is!"

From the next room, asides grated from the huge machines that spewed out small sections of memory.

"You haven't seen my apartment and my stereo system lately, you mean," he taunted her. "Alright. It's Zanny, not Ralph who eked out the information that we're repressed. It's a terrible waste of me but you don't enjoy *it*."

"I never talked to Zanny about *that*." Jill began explaining their conversation at an uptown restaurant but the brain-folds of her print-outs were emerging. Through the noise, she yelled that Zanny only wanted rum and Coke so they sat at the bar. Jill had Zanny recount the food she had eaten that week. Then Zanny asked Jill about her sex life as if she were referring to a menu. Jill didn't tell her much.

"Maybe you'll enjoy checking out all the interns haunting the hallways," Glenn said, coming back with her print-out. "While I get my attaché case and turn into a Ralph, you could turn into a Zanny."

Even when Jill hit him, Glenn didn't bother to look up. It was hardly the place.

Glenn moved over to another terminal and began drumming at the keys. "Read this," he said. "This is going to be a news shocker. There are patients in the hospital who have this new disease."

Of course, Ralph's surprise visit was strategy. The next day, Glenn blamed Jill for not waylaying Ralph so he would have a minute to exit the forbidden files in the computer terminals.

There didn't seem to be enough desire to make up their quarrel as Glenn, in a complex procedure, was let go because of insubordination.

After watching the campus horses, Jill walks back from the fields, covered now with snow-mold. She thinks about the meeting in their office this spring. A senior lab technologist told them about AIDS, what had become rumor in the hospital. The official news hadn't been released to the media by the AMA but the laboratories had to heighten their procedure.

Jill is still spending hours in the small hospital office when she isn't at classes or in her apartment. She mollifies herself with plans for the summer after she gets her graduate degree in nutrition.

Like the illusion of horses in the city, her mind moves to illusions of consolation. But the consummate illusion to her is the man coming down a knoll of the campus. Somehow, his medium features add up to good looks. He could stand out in a crowd even though his jeans are tidy and his jacket is earth-tone. Jill has to admire the only man she has really known in the city.

"I saw you walking. How've you been?" Glenn says in greeting. *Were the interns of interest?* is in a screen behind his words.

"Just fine. How have you been?" *No, the term _user_ is not going to flash out again.*

"I've been putting together back-to-school applications. I was just asking someone for a recommendation." He doesn't divulge *what school?* and knows he is stuck in Jill's thoughts until he answers that question.

"You'll never guess what's going on in the laboratory operator's office," Jill says.

Glenn wants to know what she knows.

"Zanny is engaged."

He looks as though the mainframe computer crashed.

"She stayed at a condominium during her winter trip to the Bahamas. Some guy from Detroit who sells hospital supplies was vacationing there. He says she's the one." She doesn't say that in Zanny's snapshot, her fiancé has a smug lizard smile like hers.

Glenn keeps staring, nonplussed. His eyes are soft hazel out here.

"Ursula is getting married," Jill goes on.

Glenn's stare is not one of amazement.

"I guess you didn't know she was seeing someone. A nice-looking man."

"Ralph probably knew," Glenn concedes.

"She has a futuristic glow about her."

They trudge steep steps, Glenn pondering. At the landing, he inquires, "Where's your destination?"

"I was at the Co-op, but they were out of Swiss cheese for quiche. So I took a walk to figure out something for supper."

"There's probably whole wheat flour there and another kind of cheese."

She thinks about this, as if the favorite she used to fix is unappetizing.

"I could have sworn you liked homemade pizza," Glenn says.

LAID OFF, AT THE PAST

After being laid off, Vronna wanders to a fabric store with the idea of sewing a suit for interviews. Her evenings are getting nervous. Blaming hayfever, she clutches at the Kleenexes in her pocket. The store with its goods draped like Grecian gowns and its long table for reading patterns has the quieting effect of a security blanket.

As a teenager, she explored the store on visits to the city. Though its tin ceiling was like embroidery, the merchandise didn't intimidate. Everything could be tumbled, unrolled into lengths across the tables. It was renowned for its affordable remnants and there were cards of buttons that were as remarkable as souvenirs.

Turning the pattern catalog pages, she realizes that she has not fitted a sleeve in several years. And somewhere, in the years of college and coming to the city, she misplaced her buttonholer. She winces at simple-to-sew suits, remembering defects in sewing projects, a misshapen collar.

She flips on to vests and skirts and then she stops at a quilt pattern, simple blocks attached to cut-out triangles. An Ohio star pattern, it could withstand blunders. Her bedspread, an embossed tasseled thing going threadbare, is inappropriate for a studio apartment.

The remnant tables are unthreatening, motley with dressy and utilitarian leftovers. It reminds her of the heap of people at unemployment, shifting their chairs out of line.

On a September night when leaves look ripped, as if trees had dishonorable discharges, she cuts spruce-blue velour for her quilt. She decided on an upholstery look instead of calico flowers. Above the radio man's rationale, she hears the shrieks of glass on pavement and then a siren delves through the neighborhood.

The telephone rings.

"Is that you, Vickie?" crackles a voice frail as pattern paper.

"No," she says to another of her frequent wrong callers. Vickie was her great-aunt's name, she felt like saying.

Vronna gathers her cut blocks from under her weak amber lights, twirly bulbs in candleholder sconces, and then she spreads them on her bed. Her bed nook is backed with double doors behind which an obsolete fold-down bed was once hidden. The loneliness of tenants, past decades of them, seems to be compounded with the old woodwork and the swollen plaster. Cat skeletons have been found behind walls. The place was intended for a bachelor who parted his hair with an oily metal comb and used a trunk to support his glass of whiskey. A man who traveled from a seaboard or one who folded away his rural overalls. This area of the city was now shabby but not rundown enough to be called inner city.

It mesmerizes her, cutting ninety-six triangles of heavy bronze cotton marbled with pine cones. After her adventure with a man she met at unemployment, the stacks of triangles are like welcomed empty days. Chivalrously, the unemployed photographer held open her shawl after more than two hours of becoming acquainted.

That felt so considerate, especially since she had agreed to a lunch date. It was at an art deco cafe and afterwards, they walked to a warehouse rented out by artists. His suite was a large beamed space clean with recent carpentry. He was jubilant at keeping it. She admired a blown-up poster of an advertisement she might have recognized from a regional magazine.

Feeling less tottery about him, she walked up his newly-built stairs to a loft, snug with chic, sheened furniture. Still, it was precarious to her, like a treehouse. They small-talked and looked through fresh glossies, models in a cult of cat-like postures.

At cast photos taken from a local theatre, she began to enjoy herself. He was sprawling and winsome. Then drilling began behind the adjacent wall, a sculptor he said. She asked about the other artists. The one who shared his darkroom died of AIDS.

The drilling resumed and she began to feel tottery again. He reached for her hand. She asked him where he lived and how long he had been in the city. Without hesitation or shame, he said he shared his living quarters with a woman.

Feeling that she was in a treehouse that could cave in from added weight, Vronna prepared to leave. He snatched her and kissed her. A floorboard sank.

When she returned, her hallway milk cupboard, another obsolete feature of the building, was hanging open. Its becoming unlatched is a point of irritation to her. Who unlatched it? Sweep, sweep, sweep, she heard from the apartment across the hall.

Counting 68 triangles relieves her perplexities. But her nose is on the drip. She grabs for Kleenex on her coffee table and instead, clutches a letter from her old boyfriend. She wonders about him as she cuts out another triangle.

The day she planned to work on the quilt batting, she had an interview. After it, she can make unpleasant faces over her filler layer, thinking about her interviewer.

His eyes drifted to her left hand as he retreated from their handshake. "More than seventy resumes passed over my desk. There was something potent about yours, Veronica."

His face looked as hard as a rutabaga. The upshaved style of his coarse hair made him seem military compared to her last supervisor, a polished but peevish man.

"You could walk to work, couldn't you?" His eyes sprang at her.

Down the blocks of cotton batting, she goes grinding with her shears. There was a time when she had plug-in electric scissors.

As they waited for his assistant, he found out that she hadn't ever supervised volunteers. The man was grim. "You haven't volunteered in this city? I've given evening time to fund drives. People who volunteer know what that is."

His assistant arrived, animated because her purse had been seized in the parking lot. The unlucky interview was concluded as they called the police.

Her hand aches. Stacked, her batting pieces look like a load of diapers. She shuts them away in a drawer.

She is sewing at her sewing machine. Late morning, a telephone call woke her, a languishing elderly voice asking for Clara.

Numerous squares of fabric, turquoise with gold ovals, have to be attached to the triangles. She switches on a public television quilting program. Georgia Bonesteel is before her, stitching with the finesse of a surgeon, the plan of an artist, and a sewing machine like a computer. At her relic Singer, Vronna feeds material with Georgia Bonesteel's zeal, the zeal she had with ritual tasks at her old job. Then she sews the wrong side of a square to the right side of a triangle. She has to use a razor blade to rip apart the dunce cap.

When she hears the mailman, she goes out to meet him, not having had any face-to-face business that week. Sweep, sweep, sweep, rustles from across the hall. The bearded carrier who greeted her in the foyer has been replaced with a man who hunches and averts his face.

Her milk cupboard is hanging open again. A burgundy button from her coat is in the cavity where milk bottles once perched. Across the hall, the sweeping has stopped. Hearing the tumbler of that door, she waits to see the unemployed reporter who lives there.

"Did you find my coat button?" she asks him.

His eyes aim at her but his answer is sluggish. "All I've found lately is the building dust. You'd think it entered through the walls at night."

She takes the batting squares from their drawer for assemblage. They stand puffy and full of air, like mashed potatoes. Wondering how long it will take them to mush down in the way of potatoes and diapers, she carefully centers one on a square of velour. It's like aligning phrases in the application letters she has been scattering around the city. After awhile, quilt blocks are strewn like sandwiches around her apartment.

November is outside, getting treacherous with frosts. The trees are haggard and knock-kneed. The wind rails above the ghost-sigh of her pipes and the thump, thump of an old man taking a hallway stroll on his walker. Then she hears buzzers activated, insistent at one apartment and then another.

While the old man totters at the back end of the hallway, his wife is beating on the front door. Down the five steps to the foyer, Vronna finds the old woman shivering in her short sleeves and in a wind that seems to have sewing tools in its hands.

A 30-year resident of the building, the old woman can't remember when she last left her keys inside. She clings to Vronna with fingers like tinder, gibbering, "So many dark windows. You'd think nobody slept here! Did I tell you, we used to have parties with the tenants here?"

"I'm home a lot now," Vronna says. "I'm just down the hall, making a quilt."

Returning from an interview, Vronna finds the old lady chatting with a middle-aged woman at the doorway of her one-bedroom.

"Mother and Dad are moving to a nursing home," the daughter says with apologetic pep. She wears white polyester hospital pants. "They'll live in the same room, just like here."

The old man wobbles on his walker towards them.

Showing them a burgundy button on her coat, Vronna asks, "Did you find this button and set it in my milk cupboard?"

The old woman shakes her head.

The old man says, "I can't get to the floor."

"There will be parties there," the old lady says.

"There will be many parties," the daughter says.

Today, there's a leaflet in Vronna's milk cupboard.

"He is coming," it says in type with seraphs. "Repent and prepare."

Hemming border material to her quilt layers, Vronna wonders what would have happened if she hadn't lived with her old boyfriend. Her needle sinks like a nail into the cloth.

On her way to mail a letter expressing her willingness to do volunteer work in her field, Vronna runs into a woman who lives upstairs. Her neighbor carps about her Christmas sales clerk pay, her college degree. They agree, past their spite, to make a Thanksgiving meal. Vronna buys two Cornish hens at the supermarket.

She displays her quilt on her bed, the twelve panels of spruce-blue velour with the chromatic turquoise and bronze cottons. She hasn't yet attached the bottom layer of beige fabric.

"You could sell that quilt," her neighbor says.

"It's from a pattern. Do you sew?"

"Not since junior high Home Ec."

After they eat in the dining niche, she says again, as if quilts are scarce, "You could sell that quilt."

Vronna knows that if a block of it was a resume, she would never get an interview with a follower of Georgia Bonesteel. She also knows that her neighbor is broke.

As her friend knocks with leftovers at the unemployed reporter's door, Vronna asks her, "Did you find my coat button and put it in my milk cupboard?"

"I would have mentioned it."

Sewing her assembled quilt is like trundling furrows of a field with ancient equipment. She gets increasingly nervous about sewing a stray corner in with her three layers. The entire spread, folding and falling to the floor, is an unmanageable deluge around her.

She hears wailing, a voice dismayingly near. It leaps up and down a hill of tones. She stops stitching. At first she thinks the voice is coming through the pipes, like the sounds of humming and scraping, sounds like wraith bachelors shaving. Then she fears she is going crazy. Even when she realizes that the cadence is Native American, the voice of an elderly man, floating like smoke from a campfire.

She sits in her quilt, piecing the sounds with the apartment building. In the basement lives a young man who looks Indian. He wears his long hair in a ponytail, works in a factory, plays rock music, and has people over.

"Hii-yaaaa! Aie-aaahh," the old tribal voice croons as she leans towards her sewing machine bulb. It has the luminosity of a stick match.

At dusk some days later, she goes out to mail a letter to her family. It states that she won't be home for Christmas. She's dismal enough to be nostalgic about her old boyfriend. The snow is languid drifting, and on return, she finds her building hall in a blackout. Inside, she gropes past the entry stairs to the first door, a new tenant's, and knocks. A muffled female voice answers, "The circuit's out. The owner's not home yet."

The wall leads her down the black tunnel to her door where she feels with her key. Her lights come on.

Preparing for a secluded evening quilting, she selects a needle with a large eye and a long shaft from her sewing basket. The door buzzer startles her and the needle has stabbed at her finger. Dully, she sucks her skin while the buzzer shrills again. Her hope about fuses is squelched. She looks down the crypt of the apartment hall and sees a silhouette in the snowy background.

Grudgingly, she plugs the lamp in a socket nearest her door. Then she sets the lamp in the hall where it sends beams along the carpet.

The buzzer blares again as she creeps into shadows. Like a specter with dusty hair, her old boyfriend stands at the door.

"Hello!" she says, letting him in.

"What's going on here?" he asks.

"The circuit's out." They stagger toward the corona of her lamp, too dumbfounded to guide each other.

"I called and you weren't home, so I dropped by. Dead tired," he says. He is in town for his grandfather's funeral, not an unexpected event.

She has fished the lamp from the hallway and then sits in her straight-backed chair, a cane relic, so she can see him slumped in the comfy chair.

Under the amber candle bulbs, he seems stymied at her bedsitting rooms and her slack housedress, a long gunnysack of a sweatshirt. "A small shrine. Why did you move into this place?"

She explains that it costs what she paid at their duplex. Though his grown beard and the burnish of his suede vest tell her that his work is agreeing with him, she confesses her lay off. "These were called bachelor apartments when they were built," she says.

As if reproached, he glowers at the old bedspread on her bed, now a cornerpiece of her apartment. They falter as they talk about themselves. Like dreams she's been having about her quilt, this is neverending, muddled, and repetitive without getting anywhere. She goes to the kitchen where she pours some wine. Then she wonders if he'd like a grilled cheese sandwich while she's at it.

Eventually, he dredges an unfamiliar gold-lidded pocketwatch from his vest pocket. "I promised my parents I'd be getting back." Pulling his coat on, his eyes flicker at her bed and its familiar tasseled spread.

She lights a candle. "I'll walk you to the door."

"I can find my way out," he says. In the lapping of the candlelight, he kisses her on the forehead, a restrained kiss as outmoded and untelling and strange as wax seals on old letters.

She is setting the lamp on the hallway floor, but a few steps and his coat vanishes into the dark passageway.

When people are trimming Christmas trees, Vronna spreads her completed quilt on her bed. Like a tinseled spruce, the velour is soft and the bowties made from the triangles are like ornaments. She admires the design though the diamond insets in the star pattern seem to stand out boldly. And there are small gaps in seams that she has to handsew. They'll probably look like scars.

At last, she pulls her bed from the wall to arrange the quilt borders. Plaster that waffled and cracked sifts with dust along the floorboard. She sweeps. When she takes the dustpan to the garbage, she almost tosses out a clouded penny. Thriftier now, she looks at it. On one side, she sees pillars and the worn words: ONE CENT. She turns the penny over and makes out the date beside the indistinct profile: 1910.

A 1910 penny might have paid for thread that would last through a week's labor.

THE STRANGE AND THE DÉJÀ VU

Her impulse was as strong as words on a road sign. While Hildy crept to the curb on tire tiptoe, she felt she should park in another neighborhood. Her used yellow Capri wasn't familiar to anyone at her parents' house for Memorial Day weekend. She hadn't been there for two years.

It wasn't Bruce's Cutlass swishing in. There wouldn't be an elephant yell and his arm groping through the front doorway like a trunk.

But Hildy was more emphatically what she was when she lived in the house of her parents. A two and a half story white-sided house, the kind cameras panned in the fifties for a family film. She had accepted that as she accepted the ossified red-brick school buildings she attended.

The house's façade was different. Its shutters were painted flag blue and the trim was the color of Juneberries. But their Juneberry tree, the valance to the sideyard, was gone.

Serpentine, the walk to the house. Hildy wouldn't have called it that when she cut across the grass under the basswood tree. Still there. But the garden was repopulated. The rows of tulips were gone; there was no sign of the hyacinths. Azaleas were in their place and, as little plastic posts announced, bellwort and cow tongue.

And the fritillaries were gone, what Hildy called sleepy tulips.

A few taps, the "Hello?" of a neighbor at coffee time and Hildy was staring at a strange wall. Graduation pictures, the seven portraits to the left of the entryway, had been moved. Hers with the face upswept for an indulgent photographer, had given way to a pontoon with children at the railing. The children looked somewhat like those in snapshots of nieces and nephews, children Hildy hadn't seen in person. Beside the photograph was a sampler sewn with the alphabet.

"Marlys? Oh, it's Hildy. You're early!"

Her mother had always worn a pincurled pageboy. Now she wore frilly bangs, and her hair was pulled back into a pug ponytail.

Hildy stood there instead of embracing her mother and asking about the fritillaries. "Mom, your hair looks nice. It's different."

"I was wearing this style the last time you saw me, wasn't I?" Her mother seemed to be matching a conversation with a face.

"No, you weren't." Hildy was visitor-resilient. "Did everyone arrive OK?"

"They're in the backyard, relaxing. I suppose you'll want to too. After your joyride from the city."

That was what Bruce called it. Hildy didn't savor long car trips because of motion sickness.

"Where did this sampler come from, Mom?" Hildy wondered. Then she absorbed the sight of unfamiliar living room furniture.

"I meet with a group from our local literacy chapter. We chat in English. A Japanese plant opened in town, you know. Some of the women join me to sew samplers." Her mother was two-generation Dutch. Poffertjes, her little puffy pancakes, wooden shoes on bookshelves, photographs of Hildy's grandmother with a bonnet flip had embellished their home life. Hildy's father's family had been too long in America for any cozy customs to be connected with them.

Hildy admired another sampler, stitched in oriental characters. Then she sat on the new couch that had velvet bells all over it. When it crimped, the bells cracked.

"Any coffee?" she coaxed. Her mother always had coffee ready for her and Bruce.

"There's instant. And loads of lemonade because of the grandchildren."

"Made with sugar." In Hildy's last conversation with her mother, she reasoned away her weight loss. But she reduced sugar in her diet because her dental visits were nearly as deadening as the visits to her divorce lawyer.

It was the same conch beige up to the second floor and down the hallway to her old room. Instinctively, Hildy listened for the sea sounds of breathing and heard her own exhalation at a double bed with brass bedposts and bags piled on it. She might have walked into the wrong bed-and-breakfast room. Disappeared were the twin beds from which she and her sister and then she and Bruce had kidded. Another sampler was above the bed, bright with the words, "Two hearts can beat after one drummer." A floss boy with a drum marched beneath the saying.

A breeze of voices bloated up from the yard. At the window, Hildy could see them, drawn from the winds as sailors are drawn to a harbor. A festive fraction of her family. Her brother from Seattle and the children she hadn't seen. The woman near him was his common law wife now. There was a catalog-handsome man in drawstring pants, his hair blown about a headband. He was probably her sister Saundra's husband and maybe it was their boy, standing near Hildy's father with a magazine. Strange. She could see that it was a comic book. Comic books had been banned at this house after her father said they made children into pagans, disrespectful of adults who had to strain their mortal capacities.

"Hildy! Hi!"

Was she hugging her sister for the first time in the room they shared together?

"It looks as if life is agreeing with you," Hildy said.

Instead of Marlys's clothing being an optical collision with her surroundings, she was wearing a flamboyantly feminine outfit of nautilus-pink: a shift with ferny peach-pink lace, peach-pink sandals, and sunglasses with peach-pink frames.

"Didn't Mom tell you that you're staying on the third floor? Dad didn't seem sure of your coming in his e-mail. I think he's still getting used to his mouse. Anyway, Barry and I just tossed our things here."

This sounded like Marlys with a hoard of Halloween candy.

"Barry?"

Marlys displayed a diamond ring with star points of pinkish opals. "We've been courting. I like that so much that there's no *when* to the wedding yet."

Coming from Marlys, this was surreal. Hildy had once been careful not to repel Marlys with the banality of the wedding ring she no longer wore.

"How wonderful," Hildy said.

"There's Barry. I'm showing him the Midwest." Marlys pointed fingers that once were encumbered with occult rings. Visible at an angle were her eyes, eyes that hadn't seen much of the Midwest for well over a decade.

A man in a golf shirt and yellow plaid shorts, slack as a kilt, was entering the group in the yard. He had a Bruce-ish in-shape swagger.

"He's Californian?" Hildy mused.

"He's so Californian that he's conservative," replied Marlys. "Look, he and Dad are old friends already."

"I guess I'll take my things upstairs," Hildy said. "That way, no one will be disturbed when my alarm goes off."

"You're getting up early?"

"Probably to take a walk. I've kept that up mornings since my newspaper route."

"Alone?"

It pulled like taffy, Marlys's pity. "Not so early now. After six.
Remember the dreams I woke you out of? The one about Piggly Wiggly
being held hostage? And the cops wanting a picnic."

"I must have a memory block, Hildy. I left a lot behind when I
went to Colorado."

Fights with their father, Marlys's goading him into cussing and
calling her names so that she could call him a hypocrite, then a hippo
patriot. The last of a high school sit-in for an unregulated dress code, she
called a policeman the son of a sow and went to court. After graduating,
she drove out to Colorado in a yellow hearse with a guy who dropped
into his hometown and compelled Marlys to admit that she hated her
family. "I met Bruce." Marlys's voice ripped like taffy.

"When we visited you. We got to watch you on TV,
demonstrating for abortion choice." Marlys laughed at Bruce's
department store plaid shorts.

Marlys briskly began hanging up shirts from a suitcase strewn
open upon the bed. "So much is in the past, Hildy. I've learned not to
look back." Taking super strides, according to their father's email.
Marlys was working through a late degree or two without having any
prefab ideas about loans.

Hildy had hoped for unction, for understanding about the past in
her old room. She was going to receive some comfort for saying why she
divorced Bruce. Men are mean, was Marlys's keynote. She had no
reverence for romance. Marlys attended break-ups the way other people
attended weddings.

"He's such a gentleman, Barry," Marlys was saying, her arms
encircling the window. "It's started to sprinkle and he's holding the
picnic table umbrella over Mom's head. He's walking her inside. Those
new bangs are really *her*. Barry's very calming. He works for a company
that designs burglar alarm systems."

Hildy won't tell about her divorce now. How Bruce used to
browbeat her and with enough booze during her freelance work, it
became physical. A tempting piece, he said, so tempting that you sneak
around like your old man. And the next day, he said he thought it was
just his grip that left her skin smudged violet. At least she could send in
articles.

And then, the absolution.

Hildy's mother couldn't hear it out. Spare me the instant replays,
Hildy, she said. It's not the Hildy I know. It's not the Bruce I know.

Downstairs, Hildy greeted the brown-haired children, her brother's or her sister's. But they all whizzed before her. Her brother had to call each of them by their play identities or they wouldn't acknowledge him. Between each other, they had changed their names. Curtis was Tom, Jim was Rex, and they called Hildy "Aunt Lois."

In the new living room, Hildy sat between her father and her brother, drinking the sugary dregs of lemonade. Her brother, gray and governmental from years in a social welfare office, didn't remember his old joke, "How's Dad?" As if she was next in line, he inquired, "Are you still on a work search, Hildy?"

"I have a job, as of ten months now. On a suburban county newspaper," Hildy reminded him. That was in her last Christmas card.

"You do?" He sounded skeptical and began paging through an X-men comic book. "A steady paycheck? It's not freelance, is it?"

"I've got copies in my car. I've been doing a series on daycare." Hildy was getting used to producing proof of her statements.

"That must be hard for you. Don't you have some background in grant writing? It seems like you were waiting on something at the big zoo."

Bruce took a public relations job at the zoo, before their divorce came through.

"Daycare isn't difficult," Hildy said.

"You'll get back into what you like. A more cushy lifestyle," her brother augured, closing the comic book and blinking across the room at his common law wife.

Martha was learning a sampler stitch on an old handkerchief. Her cooperation was furtive, the way she had been in Seattle when she introduced Hildy to her pastor. Pregnant with her first, Martha had Hildy solicit the clergyman's opinion about baptizing babies born out of wedlock. Afterwards, Hildy amplified on that for an article on the subject.

Martha was cooing now. "Did the Christmas sweater fit?"

"A little tight," Hildy teased out the truth. "I take a medium." She gave the disco-clingy sweater to Goodwill, shuddering at what Bruce would infer if he saw her wearing it.

"How was the sweater I sent you?" Hildy's mother joined in.

"Comfortably large," Hildy said cheerily.

Hildy didn't have to hover over Marlys's conversation with their father. That used to be like watching two marshmallows over a campfire. If Hildy wasn't attentive, she might be confronted with frazzled exteriors. Today, they were merely marshmallows with each other while Barry warmed his hand on Marlys's.

"It's doing wonders for your mother, you girls coming. A few years back, when she had fibrillations and was in bed three, four hours of the day, there wasn't much family comfort," her father was saying.

During those years, Hildy's parents called her for every minor holiday. Depression, desperation, and corns had also ailed her mother. Hildy was probably the only one of her siblings to know of the fishing affair her father was having on weekends with a divorcee. She hadn't been summoned up much since her own divorce.

"It was hard for Mom, the empty nest," Hildy interjected.

"Eh? Did you say something, Hildy? She's gotten so busy in the city, exposing old men, I suppose. Cub reporters can grow into she-bears." Her father was frazzling at her now, his eyes glinting like fishing tackle. She hadn't any plans to expose him.

"I'll call about renting an outboard motorboat. How many want to water ski?"

Hildy might have mistaken the accent of Saundra's husband for English if she didn't know he was eastern. She left her chair with the bells to sit on his. Her mother and older sister, discussing daycare, surveyed her as if she should explain why she had come to their side of the room.

"I guess I'll ask Martha about that," Saundra said. "Hi Hildy."

"Hildy, have a coconut cookie," her mother said.

"No thanks." She never ate coconut. "You're going to watch water-skiing?" Saundra used to scorn it as a status sport. She never cared about getting a suntan either.

"The kids get a thrill out of it," Saundra, previously Sandra, said in her acquired eastern accent.

"You used to say it reminded you of girls glorying on parade floats," Hildy remarked.

"I wouldn't say that." Saundra's tone was so flounced that Hildy almost believed she had forgotten her earlier feelings. They must have trickled away with about fifteen pounds that she maintained in high school.

"Did you see *Shakespeare in Love*? The costumes were stunning," Hildy small talked. Saundra studied costuming in college and was proud of doing clothing for plumped up, plumy periods. After she took a nanny position on the east coast and stayed to scrounge in theatre, Hildy rarely saw her. And then a man who worked for an importer of East Indian fabrics persuaded her to dispense with a Midwestern wedding and gown. Even as a reporter, Hildy never found out why he wanted a simple wedding and then, after they had three children, there wasn't any reason to ask.

"We saw it," Saundra said. "The husband didn't think it followed Shakespeare's life."

"I love your little girl's sundress. Do you sew her clothes?" Hildy hoped it was Saundra's little girl who was wearing the tropical scales.

"Children want readymade clothing these days. They'd rebel. I haven't sewed much for years, Hildy." Tranquil she looked, without bitterness.

Hildy's mother added, "She won't sew a sampler with me. Don't you want a coconut cookie, Marlys?"

Her mother was still saying the first name that came to her head.

"Mother, I never ate coconut. Marlys likes it. So what else are you going to do while you're here, Saundra?"

"We were down in the city. We went to the zoo, and the husband visited Pier 1 Imports and Global Village. We couldn't figure out where you live. I keep telling him how the Midwest is such a safe place to raise children. There might be more internal violence that isn't apparent, of course. I don't think all people are naturally parents. Do you think that paternal and maternal instincts are a given?"

When Saundra used to offer her opinions, Hildy felt as if she were zooming up from water for a tow around a lake. She had enjoyed Saundra for her practices at sophistication.

It was hard to believe that Sandra lashed her and Marlys with metal zippers in this room because they draped her sewing fabric over a toy eight ball. The four boys, after eating sausage pastries in the kitchen, were snapping their way out with wet dishtowels. They met with their father's tongue-lashing but when he found that their household tasks were done, he had to pronounce them free.

Craving coffee, Hildy also wanted to take a walk. She stood up and said so. The others looked at her as if she were embarking on a long excursion. No longer a family possession, she was free.

"Goodbye Hildy," her brother said. Ten years ago, 1988, January rain runneling down windows at the Seattle railway station.

"Bye Hildy," Marlys said. At the San Diego airport about five years ago, 1993.

"See you," said Saundra. At the curb near Bruce's duplex, 1989.

"Bye Doll," her father said. At the window of Bruce's Cutlass, two years ago.

"Bye Aunt Lois," called the brown-haired children.

She had walked into her parents' house and found strangers there. Years of saying goodbye had culminated in a child's nightmare. It took several blocks of her old newspaper route before she felt that she could report again on what might turn into fickleness or lies.

Her brother avoided vows because he didn't want to be a politician in his personal life, he said.

Someone would probably be moving into Bruce's duplex. Memory was not a modern virtue; it was an inconvenience.

Going past aging houses, Hildy walked in a toothache of time. People needed bridges into relationships. To get through life, they got dentures to replace pasts.

But it was just people moving in and out, from here to there, that capped the chipped houses with paint and shingles. There were pastel scooters in what used to be a spinster's yard. At a house that had altered its obstacle course of tricycles and toys daily, a second doorbell was installed above a secure vase of crocuses. Oriental children smiled at her. A man from whom she collected newspaper money bent his face blankly towards her before backing out of his driveway. The cafe where she meant to have coffee was a tire outlet.

She concentrated on spirea going profuse, bluets timid along lawn borders, lilies-of-the-valley, the immobile plants that gave ephemeral announcements like those in newspapers.

When the ache subsided and she was happy that it didn't have to be about Bruce, she was wandering toward the end of her old paper route. She didn't know when she had last seen the avenue she was shambling. It came to a cul-de-sac, hedged with the closed quiet of a courtyard. In that square area was a house she had seen in every city neighborhood she had walked, a house she skipped on her newspaper route here.

There was another dimension about this house, a ducking from the world. Its door was inset and unadorned. She paused for her bearings because it looked like a back door. In fact, the unassuming brick bungalow seemed to have two side doors. There was something about it that was dear, that daunted the passerby from thinking it modest. This one had square tiles, pearl and teal-colored, in a collar under its green shingles.

On walks in city neighborhoods, she found such a snug house, built for individuals, not an income level. She thought of buying a house then. But today, her impulse was to take the brick walk to its front garden. A sentinel of fritillaries checkered the flowerbed near the doorstoop.

Hildy thought about her brothers and sisters growing single-minded in distant neighborhoods, their long-term memories permeated with other thoughts.

It was the end of the fritillary bloom and Hildy must have drooped her head like a fritillary, looking at the flowers. The deep-set doorway opened and someone was saying, "Hildy, how are you? You're on your old route, aren't you?"

Hildy was standing in grass and as she quickly sidled to the walk, her foot tripped at a small trench beside it. Imp of impulse.

"Hi!" Hildy called after she'd righted herself. Mrs. Nowell's mouth was ruled with an ironic puncture that couldn't really be called a dimple. "Mrs. Nowell!" There had been no reason for her to know where the woman who did the subscriptions at the local newspaper lived. "I hardly ever see fritillaries."

"Well, come in and have some coffee. I haven't talked with you for ages," Mrs. Nowell said. Because her eyelids drooped, the irises of her eyes seemed to smile.

Through the door, Hildy felt a jabbing pain in her ankle. She was going away into the moment that was receiving her.

Mrs. Nowell's voice was echoing about coffee from a narrow hallway as Hildy rubbed the eyelids of her memory.

"You went for chocolate-covered cherries, didn't you?" Mrs. Nowell's voice echoed again from the hallway, patching the past on the present. She kept boxes of chocolate-covered cherries in a metal drawer below the subscriptions desk. Somewhere in this house, there used to be an antique lie detector.

Hildy surveyed the bric-a-brac, dwarfish like the house, and the fireplace, feeling the warp of déjà vu.

"So you got away from the newspaper for the weekend." Mrs. Nowell was setting the coffee and a box of chocolate-covered cherries on her coffee table. Her accuracy was almost impertinent. Hildy might have quit her job yesterday.

"How did you know that I'm back at a newspaper?"

"I saw the newspaper when we were down in the city. I read your report on that awful incident, the doves shot at someone's dovecote. The daily wouldn't pick up something like that. I've got it here, the May 16 edition."

Hildy nodded her head toward the floor, like a fritillary. She had dropped the hyphen and her ex-husband's name from hers.

"Do you still do subscriptions, Mrs. Nowell?"

"Yes. There are more female carriers now. Such big girls. I'll never forget your coming in and asking to be the first girl carrier. And the boys were hard on you, especially when you weren't getting complaints about papers being stuck in hedges or muddied up in gardens. Now they've gotten hard on me, insisting on seeing our old lie detector. I can't just joke about it anymore. Bernie's about ready to get rid of it. Aren't you going to have a chocolate-covered cherry?"

It almost sickened Hildy, her empty stomach wanting the treat and its being too rich right at the moment. She might drown in the déjà vu. There was a sense of defeat at Mrs. Nowell's remembering so much about her. The coffee's sardonic flavor helped.

Mrs. Nowell was peering at Hildy's ankle. "Hildy, your ankle is bruised."

Hildy was awkwardly resting the ankle in the slope of her other ankle, not knowing that the twist she took had pre-determined a swelling. "I guess I twisted it. I was just walking on it."

"Let me get you some ice. I can drive you home if it's getting worse. Remember the day you staggered into the newspaper office after Mr. So-and-So was drunk at his door? You said his hunting dog must have been his drinking buddy. You fell from his steps and then Howie, who was heavy for his age, stalked in and stumbled on your foot. And then when I got you home, there was such activity at your house." Mrs. Nowell's irises seemed to be grinning again. "Your father kept sending one of the others upstairs to explain about your sprain because your sister wouldn't open your bedroom door. Such a big family. One of your brothers was hauling belongings inside, back unexpectedly from school. And your mother was frantic about cherry bombs going off in the clothes chute. It was only April, I think. Well, everything's illegal now. I don't suppose they would remember that day. You just sit here, Hildy, and tell me about everything since you graduated from this town."

Mrs. Nowell had elevated Hildy's ankle to a pillowed footstool and her voice was echoing again from the corridor.

They were facts, spinning like spokes until movement and energy had conquered them and they had surpassed comprehension. Turbulence around a still spot, perhaps the source of déjà vu. A turbulence that couldn't keep truths. Most of the facts that whirled didn't matter to this moment, finally. She would be helped into a blue Buick and sit as the stationary person in her parents' household for a day, how long?

BLIZZARD AMBUSH

Because Grimson didn't usually falter at talk, he prodded Neil with questions short as those in foreign phrase books.

"T-treacherous?"

He was cold but he wanted to know about glaciers in Norway. Ice fishing, Grimson was afraid the lake outside might be treacherous in March. They were northwest of Minneapolis and their college. Grimson and Neil were crouching again, now at the fireplace in the unheated cottage that Neil's grandfather built. Grimson baited the fire with birch bark, paying attention to anything that might take his mind off thawing.

Neil was cautious with his college friend, hoping for a room in the off-campus house that Grimson had leased for next year. During their stoic meditation out on the ice, Grimson showed his fang tooth. He might be disgruntled now but he couldn't move his mouth.

Grimson wasn't even commenting on the brown plaster Indian face that was set in with the stones of the mantel. The year before, 1973, he was involved in a marathon debate after the news of Wounded Knee, the re-enactment of reservation tragedy. The debate was a draw because the people listening fell asleep after a keg of beer.

Neil said, "The glaciers can be so treacherous that if they crack, icicles as long as waterfalls crash down. The girl I was with heard one booming. I walked on a glacier and it was all ropy – as if the river was zapped solid."

"The girl?"

Before going on about the girl, Neil went to stoke the kitchen woodstove. He returned with a coffeepot of steaming water, poured himself a mug of instant coffee, and then paused while Grimson poured himself some brandy.

"I met her in southern Norway. Not in Oslo. I just wandered around there, feeling as if I'd arrived everywhere at the wrong time. Jet lag, dusk until 2 a.m., nonchalant women. I was so dazed that I went to the art museum. But the paintings of Krogh made me feel as if I were going to meet someone.

"I hadn't talked to anyone about much besides the time and the food. I ate recurring dinners of veal, boiled potatoes, and bland cabbage cooked with seeds. Finally, I went to Bergen for more of it. I have relatives on my grandmother's side there. I didn't know much about my grandfather's people except that they settled in South Dakota.

"I walked through Bergen, thinking, this is socialism. It's a fairy tale place, one where the poor quick kid got his share of the castle. I didn't see any houses that you might call your castle. After getting directions at a hostel, I ended up on the porch of my only known relative – Gunnarsen.

"My cousin was an audiologist and he kept lowering his voice while we were talking. He probably thought I had an American blare. So I concentrated on the strong Norwegian coffee and the braided bread. Then another cousin came over, Ilse. She attended the University of Oslo during the school year. She said she would show me Bergen. I felt as if I'd caught the fish that gives every wish."

Neil slurped his coffee, having reached his limit for a monologue.

He recalled how he didn't tell the Gunnarsen's that his budget included their house as his accommodation in Bergen. He'd given them the assurance of an affluent American. They remarked on the color of Neil's eyes. He explained that he was wearing blue contacts but his eyes had green in them. The color of a fish that had gone exploring on the Gulf Stream, his Norwegian relatives agreed.

Grimson set out packages of sausage, roast beef, and bread, wearing a blanket over his long underwear and his wool sweater. His wool pants were de-icing at the fireplace.

Neil began looking for the duffel bag that contained mustard and stony brownies.

Instead of asking more about Norway, Grimson was staring into the yard with the alert look of the Indian on the mantel. "Neil, why is that Indian on the mantel?" he finally asked.

Past the lacquered logs between which mortar seeped like adipose tissue, wafts of snow were stirring. Then Neil saw the snowy owl that Grimson was watching. It was perched on a stack of wood in the lean-to shed.

"Looks like that owl is gazing at the Indian on the mantel, doesn't it?" Neil commented.

"Why is it there?" Grimson asked again.

"The owl?" Neil laughed. "I'm not sure about the Indian, not even whether it's Lakota or Ojibwa or Sioux. I was about ten when my grandfather died. He never told me much about his childhood. He was just a kid during the Wounded Knee massacre."

"He never said anything about it?" Grimson was incredulous.

"He only let me know that he didn't think much of me playing cowboy." Neil switched on the radio, remembering his grandfather's scorn at his cowboy shirt and holsters in that very room. "I'm wondering how low the temperature is going."

A weather forecaster seemed to stammer through static. "The wind is up and snow is on the way. Three inches are expected from the west by morning."

"Better eat," Grimson reacted. He was still shaking his head, but now he seemed to be showing his disapproval of the room too. Its décor consisted of an old pump organ, a wall hanging of a Scandinavian boy and girl flirting across a fence, and striped coverlets on the divans that also served as single beds.

Grimson opened a can of corn and shook it into an enamel camp pan. He was purposeful rather than careful about how the corn fell. Though prone to starting disputes about issues like Wounded Knee, he looked lethargic. He was just under six feet, like Neil in build, but his fashionably unbarbered hair was brown, coarse in texture. Neil's Scandinavian complexion would become roseate near the fireplace. They set their skewers for cooking the meat and bread like ice fishing poles at the hearth.

"So what happened with the girl, Neil?" Grimson asked, pouring Neil a brandy and water.

"First I did the town. Going everywhere with Ilse's crowd, I mean. The Norwegians seemed short with me when I was on my own. But these guys were like Americans with potato chips when they got going on an issue."

Neil went mute, remembering Ilse's rejoinders to his exuberance at seeing the night skyline. It was flecked with opal gulls and gull-bright sails on the sea, amber in the dusk. Her failure to flirt, to blandish him the way women might at a Grimson kegger, made him as somber as the four dollar beers did.

It wasn't anything to tell Grimson although he was baiting him like the Norwegians had.

"The Norwegians, especially this guy named Trygg, started in on me about America. We went to a bar after seeing Eugene O'Neill's play, 'A Long Day's Journey into Night.' I couldn't help laughing at how the

Norwegian actors played people feeling their drugs and alcohol, not people hiding their effects. But then, I don't understand much Norwegian.

"I guess I said I had a great time. The next thing I was being challenged to explain the meanings of great and best. They wanted to know why America had to be the greatest and the best. Trygg explained that Norwegians are looking for contentment.

"I'm not the American embassy. And then I thought that Eugene O'Neill or another American might be the best playwright of the century. So I stayed cheerful and got up to get the next round of beer. Then this old stony guy started talking to me at the bar.

"He was babbling in Norwegian so Trygg translated. Everyone there has relatives in Minnesota, a Hansen family in Minneapolis, whatever. This man was sure I had relatives in northern Norway, where he was from. He could tell from my facial bones, he said. He was a fisherman from up somewhere north near Trondheim. Weathered and his eyebrows were like fins.

"I told him that Ilse was a distant cousin of mine. He asked me about my eye color too. Somehow I ended up taking out my contacts. The hazy fisherman looked like my grandfather then. All I knew was that my grandfather's family were fishermen. When I recalled something about the Lofoten Islands, Trygg laughed at me. Farming didn't agree with my grandfather. So I told them that the fisherman got his wish in America and became a lawyer.

"The more we joked, I was afraid that the Norwegians might throw me on a boat with Nils from the North. Trygg was laughing because I didn't know that my grandfather's family was from a latitude between Trondheim and Lapland. We'd gone out to the street. The sun was shining and it was nearly midnight."

Neil gazed at the weather outside the cabin window, reliving his worry that he would have to fish his fare to Trondheim. After he helped Ilse pay for the gas, a price as high as a tall tale, he tried the gambling machines installed in the station lobbies. He and Ilse got two lemons so often that they thought they could count on a third one rattling a jackpot for gas. To counteract his sprees with Ilse, he began buying jam, cheese, and bread, what was on all the Norwegian breakfast menus. He'd had a breakfast picnic with an American named Ann in the hostel yard.

Neil switched on the radio again. A sporadic wind was summoning wraith-like streaks of snow and this caused a butterfly net on the wall to sway like a spook's hood. The pensive owl still made a pale oval on the woodpile.

"A storm is dumping snow to the west. Winds up to forty miles per hour. Travel advisory tonight for north central Minnesota."

A drawl had entered Grimson's voice. "Maybe we should make a da-sh for it, Neil. It's less than an hour to town. That snowy owl looks as if it's fro-zen."

"If the visibility's bad, an hour could turn into three hours," Neil said.

Either Grimson winced from his brandy or because Neil was comfortable, slouched in jeans and an elk ski sweater. "Well, I probably won't find refreshing the excursion I have to make to the pot on the porch." He pulled on his parka.

On return, he muttered, "I guess the owl's not frozen."

Neil hadn't seen it jump up and shake out its wingspread when Grimson threw out the contents of the old chamber pot. It had resumed its post in the woodshed.

Neil had been sorting out the storm and suggested, "We'd better drive the car out to the main road. If we wait until morning, we could get stuck."

"There's not a fourth of an inch on the ground yet." Grimson was embracing his blanket and hot brandy. "I haven't finished eating yet. I want to know why that Indian is on the lookout here. And you still haven't told me about your girl in Norway." He had a parcel of popcorn which he spilled as he peered past the window.

"Probably it's not much more significant than the Indian in the cigar store."

"You were there when I got into that argument with Marty, weren't you? We agreed that the 1973 Wounded Knee was movie gunslinging. Then I said the Indians should have been integrated when Marty thought they should have been given a state. I guess your grandfather took the souvenir shop approach to America. Didn't he talk about the Indians dancing to raise their ancestral ghosts? The farmers were afraid." Grimson was turning his mug. "I thought Scandinavians believed in ghosts."

"My grandfather wasn't much for rumor. He said something funny though when it was snowing. He asked me if my cowboy gun could stop the snow. Then he said, 'The only uprising out there is winter, Neil. Winter is still the warrior. Snow is the siege.'"

Grimson was pulling on his heated pants and a second sweater. He switched off the radio static. "Snow isn't an uprising, Neil. The brownies are almost thawed. What about mid-summer Norway and the girl?"

"Ilse's friends were having a get-together at a lake cottage, an hour or so from Bergen. She met me at the hostel with her car."

Neil stared resolutely at the snow as he had at the sea that day, considering the price of gas and the taxes in Norway. Ann the American was planning a cheap seaside lunch of flatbread and smoked salmon. She and a friend achieved a postcard view of Bergen, hiking the foothills. At the hostel, Neil had attempted to sell a silver teardrop pin he purchased in Oslo, but without success.

"In the countryside, I photographed waterfalls that made me feel as if I were going to a wedding. Goats were hobbling around rocks like white-whiskered old men. After some scenery that was like Minnesota, we reached a red-painted cabin on a secluded lake. I brought fresh salmon from the harbor market and Ilse made dessert pancakes with cloudberries for the dinner there.

"We got to talking about the Norwegian government providing apartments and time at home for unwed mothers. I almost felt guilty, having a third beer on someone else's taxes." Neil remembered looking for the fastest laugh he'd heard in the north. All he saw were the Norwegian men sitting deadpan. "After eating, we went fishing. Just the guys, that is. I caught a few panfish."

Grimson coughed, "Would you go through all this for a few crappies? If you didn't get a Northern pike?"

He offered Neil the saucepan of popcorn, showing his fang-tooth. "I'll bet you're one of those guys who saves money on heat because you're growing scales."

Neil was still in his sweater and jeans despite the wind slapping around the eaves and the snow harpooning its way into the clearing.

He continued, "Then we went inside where the Norwegian guys started arguing about Wounded Knee. At least the scenery was worth it. You wouldn't believe those guys. Because I was from western Minnesota, they were guilting me about it. But the late night lake and sky were like peaches and paradise while we drank aquavit. The women had taken care of the dishes. I'll bet you're one of those guys who wouldn't notice that."

Somehow, Grimson's food containers were now stacked to his right, in the territory of Neil's couch. Neil resigned himself to a dorm room for his senior year. He launched into the scene that Grimson would have wished he were there to see.

"When I looked for the women, I almost turned to stone. They were taking off their baggy clothing at the lakeshore and then they walked into the water nude. Someone was asking me a question while I walked over to the window. I guess it was bad form to watch. The Norwegian guys were demanding to know why Wounded Knee happened and why the longstanding treaties were being settled violently.

"They acted as if I had input into the problem because my parents live near South Dakota. 'Why can't you get along with the Indians there?' 'How is it that you can't live with the natives?'

"They made it so personal, as if I approved of the military involvement. I had to say it wasn't a question of getting along. I hadn't known any full-blooded Indians at my schools. I said that most Americans only knew the Indian from Hollywood westerns and that it was a tragedy how the national attention they deserved had to be in the cowboy-western mode. You should have been there, Grimson. Arguing and enjoying the view. They were about to run me though a catechism – on aquavit!"

Neil blamed the aquavit for his attempt to kiss one of Ilse's friends in the kitchen, not so out-of-order a gesture in Grimson's house. Anitra was dark and indigo-eyed but she gave him the glower.

Now Grimson was glaring at him. "That's what I said in my marathon argument! Why didn't you talk about the conflict between the Indian leaders? Didn't you remind the Norwegians that there's a civil rights movement going on? To right wrongs that happened in the way of nineteenth century European wars? Why didn't you have a cause, Neil, instead of just getting excited about the girls? You never make a risky remark, Neil. You know what you do?" Grimson addressed him with a drunken man's frank dislike. "You get into your boat and you go fishing. But go on, tell me about the girl."

Grimson hunched into his blankets, glaring at the frothy fire.

Neil concluded icily, "Ilse and I drove back to Bergen that night. But the girl who went to the glaciers with me was at the hostel. Ann. She goes to school in Iowa. We traveled together after we got to Alesund with the group at the hostel. It's too awesome to see alone – the fjords from the ferries and the glaciers."

Neil was so relieved to find that his first itinerary was affordable. He had smarted from Ilse's repudiation during their last drive together. After he tried to express his fondness for her, she explained with her glower that the Norwegian women were not trying to seduce him. His American upbringing caused him to misunderstand. She already had a misunderstanding with one of the men who drove back to Oslo.

Grimson was groaning. "So that's what you were doing in Iowa over Christmas break." Then he switched on the radio.

"Eight to twelve inches now expected by morning. Visibility too poor for any highway driving."

Grimson lugged another log to the fire, causing the radio static to crash like an icicle.

"Don't put it on yet. We've got to go out there," Neil said from the window. The snow was coming down like arrows.

Grimson went to the window with his blanket around him. "The owl's still in the shed."

"You're seeing a lot of snow out there, buddy."

"Yeah? You might actually need your ski jacket, Neil." Grimson tossed Neil's ski jacket at him and bounded back to the fire. He scraped at the firewood, ashen and specked as the snowy owl.

A geyser of smoke shot into his face as a strong gale soared above them, sealing off the chimney. Grimson pushed the logs with the poker, attempting to re-direct the smoke, but feathers floated around him. He jumped back, yelping and straining to see the Indian on the mantel.

"Grimson! You're drunk," Neil prodded him. "We've got to go to the end of the road and walk back. Or should I leave you here?"

"With these feathers? Don't you think that's strange?" Grimson was tugging on his boots. Having gotten his arms into his parka, he gripped his laces clumsily.

"My nieces collect feathers. They were probably near the mantel. Or a bird might have tried to nest in the chimney. It's about as strange as a snowy owl taking shelter in a woodshed."

Grimson sat on the organ stool, tying a scarf around his face. "That Indian. Maybe it's a reminder of victory over them."

Neil shoved a foil package of roast beef into his pocket and, pulling on his ski hat, headed for the door. "Can I call you a fairweather friend, Grimson?" he wondered. "You are really insulting when you're drunk. Just stay here."

"Why are you taking food out to a warm car?" Grimson yelled, following him.

Neil yelled through the galloping gales and the whooping winds, "There's a warrior out here. Winter and its ghosts. This is for luck."

Grimson lowered his head and ran after Neil, shrieking into the blast because Neil was bounding to the woodshed, not the car. Neil threw the meat towards the owl and then they ran from the owl's overwhelming wingspread. They were slogging in the usual blindfold of a blizzard.

"A regular ambush!" Neil said, starting the car and tossing a window brush at Grimson.

Grimson cleared the windows, falling on his forearms. Then he shut himself into the car and huddled at the heater. "A hundred headdresses and every flurry on its horse. Let's get warm."

Neil had to glower. "I don't want to push a man stuck in the road. Are you sober enough to walk back?"

"How did your grandfather die?" Grimson procrastinated.

"He collapsed from a heart attack. He was shaving in the cabin when it happened. They couldn't get him to the hospital in time."

"You mean he died looking at his own face?"

Grimson's chortle was too irking.

"Did he come out here in the winter?" he laughed.

"Oh, sure," Neil said. "Ice fishing. Deer hunting."

"And once upon a time there was a Chippewa around every tree. That's why that Indian is looking out on the land. Your grandfather was scared," Grimson said in triumph.

"I can walk back alone," Neil informed him. "Build another fire inside. We could be stuck out here for another day. How the hell are we going to get along?"

"Oh no, Neil. You're not going anywhere without me. Not when we don't have a phone or a car. You'll cross country ski to the nearest heated place tomorrow. We'd better stay together. I suppose you think you can get around like some ice-crusted specter of a Viking."

Neil lurched forward into the narrow clearing of the road. "If we get stuck, it's you who's going to have to get out and push, Grimson. Because of your condition."

NUTS AND BOLTS

A late-risen woman comes in from her backyard for another stoneware cup of cinnamon coffee. She was gazing at her love-in-a-mist or devil-in-a-bush, whatever people wanted to call them. One unfisted a blue bloom above its soft skeletal leaves. She has found fifteen times that there is nothing to do in her garden, apart from weeding. Still, she equivocates at the steps to her kitchen. At the landing, she sees her husband eating from a cookie sheet spread with snack mix. Boxes of Chex cereals that she didn't buy and a canister of peanuts are out on the counter.

"Is this for the something-to-do usual tonight?" A handful proves that her husband is as capable with her Nuts and Bolts recipe as she is. His having prepared it makes it desirable with another cup of coffee. While he rearranges a cupboard for the boxes, she keeps eating what she has seldom munched in the early afternoon of a sublime summer Saturday when there isn't anything to do.

His words are as muffled as the cereal shaking in the boxes. "I said we didn't have any plans."

"I just made plans for supper. With the old lady next door. It seemed like something to do. I have to make a marinade." She's paving her way through the Nuts and Bolts, collecting peanuts. Then she eats her heavily peanuted handful as her husband turns to her. He's wearing an old pair of chinos the color of sand dollars and a shirt patterned with small sailboats that, after many launchings into the laundry, reminds her of a pajama top. This accentuates the early silver that outlines his hair.

"I said I would go," he states. "It's at White Bear Lake tonight and there's going to be a sailboat or two."

Her hand flaps down for a few more peanuts. "Same old bunch?"

"Not exactly. The newest baby will be there and at least one of the mothers won't be sailing."

"She wouldn't sail anyway. It's her third. And that's the third baby born into the same old bunch this year. I don't think you really meant what we agreed on." She doesn't look up since she is exchanging pretzels for more peanuts on the tray.

"I haven't changed my mind. They seem to think we're happy. Are you going to stop eating that?"

"I'm just eating my portion. Really, they're getting to be a fertility cult," the woman replied and swallowed to a falsetto. "'You just

can't imagine how it makes you feel. Papa's little precious.' Proof is
what they mean and you go anyway, like a weight watcher going to eat
birthday cake or a person on a budget admiring someone's new car."

"But you know who lives out on White Bear Lake. His one kid is
long gone," the man insisted. "Look, I just said we had no plans."

"Then go if you want. You'd better put this out of sight. Cheese
balls, chips, sea salt, seasoned steak. I'll bloat up like a water mattress
right now. And then they'd probably want to push me out on one."

Nothing to do and it is the wafting weather that follows days of
haranguing thunder and rain, the humidity mounting like remorse. The
couple has decided to go for a walk. It is their first summer in their house
on the outskirts of St. Paul, near Como Lake. Only the supper with the
sailboat has to be answered somehow.

St. Paul is like a curious acquaintance that they are getting to
know gradually, unlike the bunch from the man's job that meets
regularly and makes rounds of houses. Today they have stuffed
swimwear into a bag that the woman carries. During a spell of heavy
heat, they heard about an outdoor municipal swimming pool from a
youngster across the street. Como Lake in the 1980s functions as a
mirage to swimmers and pollution-conscious people who feed the
wrong-side-of-the-state mallards.

The man and the woman stroll past houses with brick arches and
vines hanging like arras. They are still pleased with their slate-blue
stucco house and its cat-quiet rooms. With spare rooms for their
diversions, neither the man nor the woman has ever had so much space
and peace. They have both come from families where chaos, crises, and
grievances became grotesque growths in the memory. They postulated
that some of these inherent or chance-caused experiences were best not
repeated.

Newfound freedom came from that, an adulthood that had the
independence and happiness of an ideal childhood. They accomplished a
genuine dignity at home. After that, they became carefree, even spoiled.

"That's the bike that could nab the thief," the man's voice flares
in the neighborhood. A boy looks up from the silver fluorescent initials
that he's painting on the diagonal bar.

Approaching the boy, the woman says, "Alma, next door, said
that none of the alley neighbors have been able to keep a bicycle in their
garage." She smiles at the boy.

The boy's eyes headlight her as if they are ringleaders of the night force that specializes in bike theft. The woman feels cut by the sheer phosphorescence of the boy's glare. He is cleancut in cut-offs, his hair wiped away from his forehead.

Uncomfortable, the woman complains about the risk of leaving bikes unattended in bike racks. She and her husband both have new bikes that scale the basement staircase as often as they are ridden. Otherwise, the frequency of crime is so low in the neighborhood that only a few years back, in 1979, a woman reported that she offered a burglar cookies and milk before he hurried away. And people laughed at the news.

"Those are my initials, TL," the man said. He didn't mind the blatancy of the boy staring at him.

After they're out of earshot, the woman says, "Maybe the punks wear their hair so they can be identified like that bike. Their parents could say, 'The last I saw her, she had a spikeball haircut of clover green and clover red. There was a crescent moon painted on her right temple and a tattoo timepiece on her left wrist. She has four earrings possible on her left ear and three on her right ear. She was wearing chains on black."

"They are all wearing chains on black this year, ma'am. Can you tell us about her fillings?" the man rejoins.

Incredulously, they consider the close-set brick homes, a march tune to St. Paul natives but lucky for a newcomer to own. They have felt finality about the linen-like yards, about the women and the men who show their blue-noded legs, about the geraniums and the hydrangeas. Even though they saw a woman flip the bird at a man driving out of the alleyway, they know that most fighting is done secretly. They felt this in the soundproof stucco during midwinter and in the summer when cars could be heard screeching towards the sunset. But then, seeing the old bunch, they became confused, dubious about their interpretation, thinking for a day or two that there might be a better life than they had known, that they hadn't believed in something.

Something got her thinking about her grandmother. A basement window, at the height where a toddler can be a peeping Tom and see the tuba convolutions of a furnace inside. At such a window, she watched the waiting room of a local boy doctor, the self-proclaimed healer of anatomical humiliations.

Or it was the old oaks, reaching as the ones prohibited then. Children dared the wind, the neighbors, and their bodies when they climbed to the height of the house shingles. She fell from a low branch and went to a doctor who examined her sprained ankle without her having to remove any clothing.

Or it was when she came in from the yard, the three steps to the kitchen, the snack mix.

She had come into such a kitchen, anticipating lunch. Her mother, setting bread, margarine, mustard, and sliced Colby cheese on the table, murmured on such a day as this, "If Grandma comes in, don't let her have any cheese. It's loaded with salt."

While her mother was cutting carrot spears, her back turned from the kitchen table, her grandmother slippered in. She was still sturdy looking, her cheeks puffy rather than cracked, like dumplings, and her hair a silver filigree on dark gray. She could sit down without scraping her chair. Her smile gleamed like the marbled formica. She wasn't herself anymore, her mother said. She was sil-lee, enunciated like *senility*.

On seeing the skulking widow, her mother went to the refrigerator for food from an infirmary-white corner – salt-free bread, chicken boiled without salt, and salt-free butter, bland as bananas.

"Here are some carrot and celery sticks, Mother," her mother said matter-of-factly before she turned back to the counter to grab a bite herself. At mealtime, her mother would be on a diet.

The girl and her grandmother began to play pretend about a doll taking a nap. The doll, her grandmother's gift, was made from a dustmop. It had a babydoll dress of dustmop tassels and braids of dustmop strands. As she talked with her grandmother though, her grandmother pondered the plate of Colby cheese.

Eventually, her grandmother was talking to the cheese. Then she reached and lip-said, "Please pass the cheese." As she repeated that, her eyes seemed to be saying, "I'm the oldest."

It was a usual act of mealtime civility, pushing the plate of cheese towards her grandmother. But this became collusion when her grandmother slipped a piece of cheese inside the folds of her dress.

The girl struggled with her tongue, heavy as a shovel, until she finally said, "I'm going to get Moppa up from her nap." She bolted from the room.

Her grandmother was still undetected when she returned with the dustmop doll, another doll she didn't dandle much. She disliked dolls in the way she disliked naps. Both of these activities seemed to be a pretense and not for the reasons of sleep or love of a doll. She never slept during a pre-planned naptime; she listened to her mother's clandestinely-watched soap operas from a stairwell. That day she began lying too, pretending to enjoy playing dolls because her grandmother wanted to play dolls – until the other children arrived for lunch.

A few weeks after that visit, her grandmother died.

"But there's no spot on the wall to focus on for balance," the man is saying. He blinks at children screaming from their loss of equilibrium in the capsules of the Tilt-a-Whirl at Como Park.

"You won't go on the Tilt-a-Whirl? What if people want you to go the State Fair now that we live near it?"

"Look at that boy," the man says. "Look at his loss of control. I like the rides that are almost an accident but then you're saved."

A boy of about seven can't walk a straight line from his swiveling capsule. His parents, behind the cordage, beckon as if he's warped from a conflicting magnetic pull.

The woman wonders if she or anyone could wheedle her husband onto the Tilt-a-Whirl.

Round and round and round, a little girl shrills and whizzes and makes the woman smile. As the girl comes out of her Dorothy tornado, her hair fuzzed in the sun, she clutches a raspberry-haired troll man grinning like Alfred E. Neuman.

A tiered balcony view of the lake and its walkways can be had if the two loll near the mock orange bush on a knoll. Someone scraped a circle of soil and the grass around it is yellow as matchsticks. A dust of ashes is left from a defiant campfire. Mornings, Como Park is strewn with wine bottles in paper bags, empty packages, cigarettes.

There was a two-acre wood, she recalls, behind the town's last avenue, Gunthar. An old mailbox made the oak grove look like private property. The neighborhood kids who could play until dark kicked a can to signal their secret council in the woods. One evening, Moppa, the dustmop doll, was charged with witchcraft.

The neighbor girl's brother, whose name was Ezekiel Smite when he hooked buckles on his shoes and wore a dad's hat adorned with a buckle, was a witch hunter. He accosted her with questions.

"So why did you leave the table to get the doll when your grandmother had a forbidden slice of cheese?"

She answered, "Moppa woke up from her nap and was calling. I thought my mom would catch my grandma with the cheese."

Ezekiel's sister, in her eyeleted cloth curler cap, hissed out, "So how did your grandmother eat the cheese when Moppa was at the table?"

"Moppa was looking for dust," she replied. "When she saw my grandma slip the cheese into a sandwich, she said, 'There it is. Dust.'"

Ezekiel Smite began lashing a chokecherry stick at the ground near Moppa. Another boy tied Moppa's hands with one of her mop-strands.

"Moppa had been having a dream. In it, she had to find dust and lots of it. She asked a wizard where to get the dust. The wizard said, 'You know that dust comes out of thin air. Dust is the first magic. And then, things turn back into dust. Cheese is a food that gets dusty fast.' But when Moppa wanted to see if the cheese had dust on it, my grandmother said, 'Why don't you check the vacuum cleaner bag?' And then she started eating the cheese."

Ezekiel's sister, appalled as a mother whose child has mud around the mouth, demanded, "And wasn't salt bad for your grandmother? And isn't salt in cheese?"

Ezekiel Smite kept slashing at the campfire clearing.

She confessed that cheese had salt in it. Her sister sat on a low limb of the cottonwood tree, her eye gazing as a corpse's while the doctor of deformities, on another branch, munched a Snickers bar.

"She talked to a wizard! And isn't a mop, what that doll is made of, something like a broom, the sign of witchcraft?" Ezekiel Smite finished the inquiry, pointing his stick at the dustmop doll.

The girl didn't answer, regretting that she had told anyone about the cheese and her grandmother. Her sister knew Moppa was innocent, that she was gathering dust from long naps and neglect.

"I wonder if it's kids or the homeless who had a campfire here?" the man muses.

"Women have warned me about walking around the lake after sunset but they didn't tell me of an incidents," the woman replies.

"Is there time to walk to the zoo? Or is there something you're going to have to get at the grocery store? I used up the butter on the Nuts and Bolts."

"There's another pound in the back of the fridge."

The man stretches his foot under the woman's ankle, digging his heel into the circle of dirt. "You've been forgetting things lately and then someone has to make a grocery run before supper."

His head juts towards the walkways at the bottom of the slope where a mother strolls with her two toddlers on two leashes. Jaunting along on the lane behind her are two women with their urban dogs, a cockapoo and a terrier. Eventually, the barks of the dogs attract the toddlers and the leashes become entangled.

"Alma said that a beer marinade would be fine on her food. She makes jewelry and got involved with a pterosaur dig while she was out west. She said that kittens are in demand around here."

"Shish-ka-bob in beer marinade. That's pretty low of you when it's just you and her," the man grumbles.

On the knoll, a bunch of boys are playing with branches, aiming them, flourishing them, daring people to ask if they broke them off of trees. They're at the anti-heroic age when girls are taller. Then they pretend that they're stabbing at litter. The woman sees one of the boys pulling a baggie from his pocket and then blowing it up. Still reclining, the man resumes watching the trickle of people on the lake lanes. Then he notices the attention of a few passersby after the baggie is imploded behind him. He takes a desultory scan around at the boys. The one who was pretending to collect litter is dangling a condom in the air behind him and his wife.

"You little bastard!" the man reacts. He bounds up while the boy with the branch drops it and runs into a ring of laughter. Inhibiting the urge to discipline these boys, the man hesitates. He doesn't know them and is drawing attention to their ribaldry. He steps back to his wife.

"They'll get it for something," he mutters as they walk away to the pathways. The day seems destroyed, the man clenching his fury as if he is holding an overheated car key.

The polar bear exhibit is in a concrete chasm with blocks that have the dimensions of icebergs. The man first stood above the gorge and looked down at the berg-like bank on a May afternoon that had gone wet and whip-winded. Seeing another man throw something over the railing, he was diverted from leaving. Nets of rain billowed down upon the zoo.

The older man seemed to be tossing a stick-like object in fun. But reaching the railing, the younger man saw a bear galumphing after a screwdriver. Then a shower of metal nuts and bolts fell on it. The bear's tormentor, snarling something, was grasping a caved-in paper sack. He wore jeans that were matted manure-brown in places and a sweat-yellow

T-shirt that twisted above his slopping stomach. His shoes seemed to have been polished with car oil.

"Hey, cut that out!" the man yelled. "That bear's done nothing to you."

The other man's eyes were unreadable while rain drizzled his face. He still held a monkey wrench in the soggy remains of his sack.

"Yeah, you gotta protect these bears. Fun to look at, like a woman. I'm just a shift of work. Guys like you throw things at me all day and I'm supposed to protect everything except my sanity."

Shambling on down the viewing deck like a gladiator with an advantage, he raised the monkey wrench and then he flung it onto the grass. The man lost sight of him while he went looking for a zoo guard.

On the sultry July asphalt, a bear that the man calls Junior is so languid on the concrete berg that it seems to be in summer hibernation, is playing dead, or is dying.

"It makes a person want to toss something at him to see if he's alright," the man says softly, like a hypnotist.

"Did you ask if they let the bears out on the snow?" his wife wonders. She reads the sign that forbids people to throw food down at the bears.

"This exhibit reminds me of unused stairways in office buildings," the man says. "I told the guard it was a barracks."

"Ashes or dust? Ashes or dust?" Ezekiel Smite asked the witch hunters.

"Dust. Let her dust."

Though another dustmop doll could be made, the girl was regretting that she turned in Moppa.

"Dust to ashes, dust to ashes," Ezekiel Smite chanted while he tied the doll to the chokecherry branch with the tassels of its babydoll dress.

"The doll didn't do it," she said.

"The doll said the cheese was dust when it was poison for that grandmother," Ezekiel's sister said unctuously.

"We could kick her around in a can," said a boy at the cottonwood.

"Or the stocks," said the doctor of deformities, jumping from the tree's branch. "I don't have any matches."

"Burn the dustmop, for that is all thou art, as a witch, at the stake. Mop to ashes, mop to ashes," said Ezekiel Smite, a known pyromaniac. There wasn't much time, because after Ezekiel pulled a box of campfire matches from his pocket and lit one, she saw his weird determination.

The man and the woman meet at the water's rim after being separated at the turnstiles of a municipal swimming pool. They had already exchanged their clothing for a basket key when the woman realized that, its being Minnesota where lakes are within driving distance, the municipal pool is the domain of children. The woman had to hide in a stall that smelled like wet cardboard, listening to graffiti whispers, things worse than "Aunt Wiggly loves Uncle Ugly."

Draped in their towels, the man and the woman decide to sit at the pool's perimeter first and consider the screams that burst sporadically like balloons.

"Did they burn the doll then?" the man asks, watching the children make flames of the water.

"They shortened her dress. I ran off. They all knew I wanted a cat, not a doll. The boys came back shouting 'All-ee all-ee in come free' as if they were playing Kick the Can." While screams surmounted her voice, the woman looks chic in her dahlia-pointed swimming cap and her slightly streaked make-up.

The sun is intense. They can't resist dunking to their shoulders and bobbing past the birdbreasted girls and the boys skinny as salamanders. Eventually, the man falls into a drifting float nearer the deep end of the pool. His wife bumps like a frog and then she dives under where the sounds are stately and the light diffuses like streetlamps.

They can't do any real swimming. Two lanes are roped off but what they watch is go-cart uneven. One freestyle is so groping that the youngster might be reaching for candy from a clubwoman. A hot rodder passes him to be greeted at the lane's end with a traffic whistle.

Eventually, kickboards catch up with the couple and begin colliding around them. Making for their towels, the two confess that they never minded children so much because they didn't have to mind them.

Drying in the sun, the woman muses, "My grandmother used to tell my mother not to yank so much when she braided my hair."

The man's eyes have dropped to the ties of her swimsuit.

"And you also have been good to me, of course," she adds. She is gazing in the direction of a boy whose eyebrows are shaped like crochet hooks, similar to her husband's. She hasn't seen many boyhood photographs of her husband.

Somewhere, another child screams and then whistles answer in constabulary code. The metal ball in the whistle is spinning and shooting and then it tapers with the lifeguard's breath.

Strolling home, the two talk about eventually starting vines that will scale their stucco. Morning glories, the woman suggests. The man thinks purple clematis would contrast nicely. As they pass a neighbor with whom the man has discussed snow zones, bad backs, wives, and the boy who keeps his father jigging at basketball, the old woman next door appears on her steps. She looks frosty and geological. "An hour?" she calls.

The younger woman pats her hair. "That's right, an hour." But her voice sounds strapped. The old woman's pumps have square buckles on them.

"So are you going to White Bear Lake tonight?" the woman asks her husband.

"Our breeze isn't," he replies. "I'd start wanting a sailboat and then a lake. I'll keep her busy with the snack mix."

"I forgot. Alma says she goes to bed at exactly sundown in the summer. She might bring some rocks from the West with her."

Neither of them want to pout the complaint of well-fed children – that they're bored and there's nothing to do. A baby-weight cat exclaims at the door. And an old woman must be de-strangered, satisfied with shish-ka-bob, and entertained with discussions about the bones of flying lizards, treasure hunts for moss agates, and the proper habitat for polar bears. Because she will have too-definite feelings about climbing vines, they will find out how definite she feels about other things that neighbors do.

They already know how the evening will end, that they will tell her they might catch a bicycle thief, which is why they watch their garden grow past sunset. But they will have forgotten what phase the moon is in. The bright, barren, good-for-nothing moon. Out of propriety, the lawns being more visible from a darkened window, they'll wade in through the dewfall on the grass that grows too fast.

THAT NUMBER AGAIN

The week after I returned from Peru, I saw Mitchell again. I was already perplexed from my research on Inca quipus. Having studied Indian weaving, I was hoping to prove that the knots and string colors in their textile telegrams told more than an abacus did in the Orient. Inca messengers, running through the steep hills, must have had more than numbers to deliver.

For weeks, I had taken notes on tomb quipus, convinced that the knots were a Morse code that recorded personal information about the dead. In the mountains, I attempted to find coded calendars, handed down, in the weaving there. The women grew distrustful, either because they no longer knew the significance of old patterns or because I was an from North America, an unmarried woman following them while they herded llama. So I went to Ica where I could photograph the tomb quipus.

Mitchell asked me to spend the evening in a disordered apartment that he had taken the week before. Though he didn't balk at seeing me again, what he used to do when I came back from Peru, his chin dropped at my devotion to the quipus. On the subject of numbers, he told me about the day he called with the news that he was divorced.

Mitchell was feeling spooked that day because his odometer turned to 31,000 miles while he was on Interstate 35 to Duluth. He had become obsessive about numbers, he said, and the number 31 signified the worst year of his life. It was late June and Mitch would turn 36 in August. He had just delivered the final results of a 2-year newspaper poll he conducted in Northern Minnesota. Numbers had come to represent whole sentences to him.

Mitchell's superior disappointed him because he didn't have any extension of the polling work and he suggested that Mitch could connect up with market research work again.

"I'm waiting on a possible year's teaching contract at a college up north. Statistical methods in sociology," Mitch replied.

He wanted to tell about his other alternative, returning to school for his Ph.D., but the newspaper editor was gorging himself on computer sheets. Absentmindedly, he asked what the college was offering.

"It's comparable," Mitch said.

"I have a friend who got $31,000 on being tenured recently," the other man mentioned. Then he grumbled about the low percentage of people who became subscribers after being canvassed. He seemed to be talking with a full mouth when he gruffly thanked Mitch.

Feeling that he needed to be wished good luck, Mitch then called me from the lobby telephone. Afterward, on his way to Duluth, he estimated that I was 60% enthusiastic at the prospect of seeing him.

Right after his car thudded over the third animal corpse on his 3-hour drive, Mitch's odometer turned to 31,000 miles. He saw in the rear view mirror that he had run over a raccoon even though its mask had been ripped away and then he saw the numbers in front of him change in the slow, sinister way of odometers. This reminded him of his 3rd year of marriage, the listlessness of it. Even though the highway inclined into Duluth like the ring of a planet above Lake Superior, his mind couldn't rise into forgetfulness.

Mitch drove on down to London Road where he decided to refill his gas tank before going home. From the station's pavement, he could see Superior, Wisconsin, in a mist that gave him qualms about his future. He liked to count the barge-like ships in the receding light.

Mitch didn't notice the total for the gas until he was putting the gas gun back into its holder. He knew it was inane to think anything of the number 31 being in the total, $18.31. But seeing that number again made him think one of the long ships could jackknife into the lake. He wondered how much would go wrong with his Sunbird while it was on its 31st thousand miles. He even thought about changing his odometer so that it would skip the unlucky number.

When the boy at the station's cash register stated, "$18.31," Mitch was irked enough to alter the number 31 right then and there. He quickly obtained ½ gallon of milk from the dairy cooler.

"$19.87," the boy said as the cash register rang with its incontrovertible sum.

1987 was the year that Mitchell was 31-years-old.

Boys like that, he thought on his way to his car, are as stolid as messengers when they say nothing of significance. Mitch decided to drive to a restaurant where he could evade moping over the years since his more trustworthy 20s. All week, he had been immured with calculations and computer sheets, finalizing figures after his canvassers had gone. His thoughts were bent by unlucky numbers while he watched for lucky numbers that corresponded to years when he was happy, numbers that he hadn't chanced upon all day. A view of the ships and the harbor lift-bridge, latticed and luminous as a constellation after dark, would set his mind adrift even if he didn't feel blessed.

He wanted to concentrate on the decision he had to make. His impulses were directing him back to the Twin Cities, the place where he had made a wrong decision, as if he could correct it now. But he didn't want to brood over the worst year of his life and Leigh, his ex-wife. His memory of her was like a malediction.

She took 3 months of fits and starts to tell him she didn't love him. Because of her gift for trends, she was often confusing to live with. Mitch used to tell her she was dashing. The day she said she didn't love him, she had changed from a Spandex sweat suit into baggy Arabian pants. While he was taking in her confession, she put on jeans and a llama serape, what she bought when she was taking anthropology. Then she said goodbye to Mitch.

At first, Mitch thought she was acting out one of the new therapies she used in counseling juveniles. But after breaking up, she had a "survey" conversation with him during which she made Mitch admit that he was dissatisfied, as if people were product brands. When Leigh passed through anthropology, she found out the drawbacks that went with my brand of female. She pitied Mitch when I first went to Peru.

Mitch considered himself stultified, but then his mother called to tell him that his father had a stroke. The months after were excruciating since he spent them watching his father's resentment, what once focused on Mitch's opportunity to propagate numbers in an office. Now his father flared because of his recent inability to perform the most belittling of tasks. Leaving Leigh alone weekends was the catalyst for their separation. And then he, the unrecommended, walked out of the market research job that bought their house.

"Just one?" the waitress asked Mitch. She lead him through the bar area to the window he wanted. They passed kegs coming out of the wall and a mantel that supported steins with castle stairways and turrets on the fliplids.

Mitch ordered a stein of beer and looked away from the waitress's curls because they seemed to giggle at him. The water outside was paned in light, making him feel as if he were still on the road.

When Mitch became unnerved, his index finger squirmed at the sideburns he had kept since the 1970s. He asked the busboy how his table came to be the 31st.

It was in the 3rd wait station, the busboy said and then he wondered if anyone would be eating with him. Lewdly and attentively, the busboy waited for Mitch's reply, the same servile busboy that had cleared tables when Mitch took one of his canvassers to dinner. After Mitch denied a dinner partner, the busboy shrugged with the take-it-or-leave-it attitude of the Northern Minnesotans.

At Table 31, Mitch felt the stagnation of his fate. It seemed to be in the power of a featureless mastermind, a deity that reached him through numbers, marking him. Divorced, he was now in the darker patterns of sociological behavior just as fault lines are associated with the negative side of nature. Though he wanted a T-bone, he ordered onion rings and a Polish sausage sandwich so as not to be conspicuous. He wasn't heartened, seeing that the menu didn't have the number 31 anywhere on it.

When Mitchell looked across the restaurant room, he was confronted with a couple. The woman had the catkin sensuality of dates in their late 20s. She looked to be about Leigh's age when he was 31. Her bearded partner had tines of hair at his neck, as did the hirsute tree surgeon that brought spare ribs to one of Leigh's barbecues. The tree surgeon amused Leigh, quoting the laments people made before their diseased grandfather elms were hacked down. Though he looked like Leigh's brother, he provided the reason for the divorce.

Mitchell's gaze fell to his bare arm and then out towards the lift-bridge. Tonight it resembled a trellis on a wedding cake, elevated from the city where he had found only immature women to date. Easily steered and impressed, they couldn't speak to the specter that hung in their silences – the person he was before his 1st marriage.

My telephone number hadn't changed, a rumination that was not painful as Mitch sat at his dinner. Eating his blueberry pie, he made the number 823-8129 into an anagram, a combination lock of our pasts and he shared it with me when I saw him. At 23 he met me; in 1981 he said he loved me; when we were 29, he said he loved me not. And now he wanted to get to know me again.

"Rosetta, this is Mitch. Rosetta Runnell?" he had said earlier that day.

"Why are you calling?" I said.

"I might be finishing up my graduate work in Minneapolis. I've been divorced 2 years, Rosetta. I suppose you know that," he said. "I've been in Northern Minnesota, canvassing. How have you been?"

Wearing khaki shorts as usual and wary as I was the day Mitch shifted his eyes from my unshaven legs and admitted he was getting engaged, I decided not to tell him much. "I finished my Ph.D. I'm teaching an anthro course at night now," I said. "It feels like all the loose ends are hemmed under, getting a Ph.D. Now that the quarter's over, I'm going to Peru for a month, just like before. Incas and their descendents are still my passion."

"I thought I'd find out whether you would hate me if I ran into you," Mitch explained. Then he asked if he could call me again.

"You might not run into me much," I said. "We'd probably be artifacts in each other's lives."

After wondering if I still had that amazed expression and if my hair still looked glazed by the sun, Mitch guessed about the couple within his eye range. The guy thought he was a conquistador on the subject of physical love. Surveyed, he would answer that he would toss out a straying wife. He wasn't a liar but he would probably vote for a Democrat who was one. He would rather spend money on a Skidoo than on daycare. After hundreds of television commercials, he wanted the toothpaste his mother bought. He stated that he read more than a few books a year but that included manuals for machinery. He believed in God although he did not believe that God got involved in elections. He didn't think Lawrence Welk's accent was real anymore, but his girl is.

"Mitchell Jacobs," a deep voice said in the tone of one involved.

Mitch looked up to see the statistics professor he met at his interview with the sociology chairman at the college. Dr. Dastin was wearing a black and ash-colored umpire-striped shirt. It matched his mollusk-gray hair.

"Hello, Dr. Dastin," Mitch said.

Lurking nearer, Dr. Dastin turned to a woman whose gray eyes were embedded like his. "Here's the man I might be team teaching with next year. This is my wife, Tilly."

"Nice night," Mitch said.

Because Dr. Dastin was curious about Mitch's canvassing, Mitch could explain his dinner out alone. His head was spinning with numbers.

"You know what jags the mind from a repeated calculation?" Dr. Dastin said. "A game of chance." Then he invited Mitch to drop over to his house for another beer.

"It's probably out of his way, Roger," Tilly said. Sympathy softened her voice.

Dr. Dastin seemed to be feeling his evening's beverage. He had a roulette wheel in his basement, he said, for bets on chips. "It's a hobby of mine, looking at a game of odds as if there is a system other than playing conservatively."

As luck would have it for Dr. Dastin, Mitch's duplex was located on a sidestreet 2 blocks down the hill from the Dastin's.

Driving home, Mitch didn't regret taking this risk. He might not hit it off with Dr. Dastin but he should be making a decision. The professor's house, he found, was a newer design of the grandiose houses in the area. It looked as if it were in cell division. Ferns and flowerbeds were planted in neat domino rectangles.

Tilly led Mitch through a murky living room to the basement where Dr. Dastin was unfurling a cloth with betting squares printed on it. At his bridge table, he was as graceful as a magician and he wondered if Mitch liked Ravel's "Bolero," what was playing on the tape deck.

Mitch nodded with the sauntering saxophone and looked at the pictures on the green stained paneling, op art geometrics of marbles and mazes and cubes.

Marveling at Dr. Dastin's authentic game wheel, Mitch eluded his questions about the unreleased statistics for the region. "That's right. Numbers to 36 on the carousel. Nearly my age, 36," Mitch said.

"Ready for roulette?" Dr. Dastin asked. The lines on his face were as regular as grid paper. He handed Mitch a pad of paper, a stiletto-sharp pencil, a beer, and stacks of chips. Then he said that Mitch could call him Roger.

Conservatively, Mitch bet low stakes on all odd numbers. When Dr. Dastin bet, his eyebrows almost shut his eyes. He gambled on the numbers 29, 30, and 31, to Mitch's discomfort.

Then Dr. Dastin spun the wheel, his finger flaring from it like a wand. The marble swirled like something going down a drain. They both lost on the number 28.

Mitch next bet on all low numbers while Dr. Dastin bet a higher stake of chips on 29, 30, and 31 again.

The macabre marble wobbled this time before it dropped into the 29 slot. As Dr. Dastin recovered chips from the bank and took what Mitch bet, Mitch regarded him as if he were riding the wave of an evil force. Clarinets insouciantly repeated the Spanish "Bolero" strain. Mitch gulped his beer.

"Why did you bet on those numbers, Roger?" he asked.

"29 hasn't won in 400 spins of this wheel. I was beginning to think it was the wheel," Dr. Dastin replied, his eyes big as a ghoul's. "I like the number 29 the way Jack Benny did. That was a rewarding year for me."

"My 31st year was the worst of my life," Mitch said with the pessimism that hopes to be surprised.

Conversely, Dr. Dastin was 31 when he was awarded his Ph.D. "I hope your 31st year *does* turn out to be the worst year of your life, Mitch," he said and bet on number 1 through 12. Number 7 snared the marble.

"Try some higher stakes? Like to try turning the wheel?" Dr. Dastin asked and then waited for Mitch's bet with the smirk of a clam.

Mitch began to bet on straights of numbers. The three he gambled on, 10, 11, and 12, were reminiscent of summer days he spent as a boy at an outpost clubhouse. In a chess game, he won squatter's rights from a rural man who seemed capable of using his cane as a weapon.

Eventually, Mitch accumulated a few winnings, even while he bet on the trio of numbers that signified the years we were together.

"You're uncanny, Roger," he said, as Dr. Dastin began to accrue towers of chips in front of him.

"As if I had the unknown in hand. As if you don't believe that my wins are meaningless. So much is made of meaningless incident. Take your job, for example. I put my bet on you. I like your experience. In marketing research, there's not much impetus to fix results. Now the sociology chair has called me about another candidate, a new Ph.D., family man. Fair warning, Mitch."

"I'm a divorced man, Roger. Luckily, I was not blessed with children." But Dr. Dastin probably knew that already. "I don't like to think what the chair might predict about me."

Dr. Dastin shrugged and spun the wheel again. "You had an unlucky number that might not occur again, if life is anything like roulette. Who could put their money on the married people these days?" The unknown sociological factors, according to Roger Dastin, were the thinking man and the thinking woman.

"I'm betting on my 36th year, single number bet," Mitch announced before he took the last slurp of his 2nd beer.

Dr. Dastin had begun betting on pairs, his sunken eyes wide and dank. But he lost as the marble swung into the 29 space.

"I'm feeling less conservative," Mitch said, feeling the 3rd beer. His heap of chips was dwindling while Dr. Dastin had maintained his little fortress. Mitch bet on 36 again.

As the marble went around in circles, Mitch thought about the chips being money and how he would bargain with something omniscient for a blessing. Knowing that if he didn't win soon, he would owe the bank, Mitch sacrificed on 36 again. He watched the numbers of his past, the years of his life so far, revolve into streaks swirling like blood in the black chars of time, the marble trundling against them.

Dr. Dastin, after betting on the trio 31, 32, and 33, had an infernal look of triumph. The marble landed on number 31 and the "Bolero" trumpets shrieked. Mitch couldn't tell how many times the theme had played.

Shaking with frustration, Mitch said he had had enough for the evening. He thanked Dr. Dastin for recommending him to the sociology chairman and bounded back from the roulette table. But then his foot slipped on a rug fringe. The linoleum must have been recently polished and the surface of a leather chair was slippery. Mitch fell to the floor.

"I'm still betting on you, Mitchell," Dr. Dastin said as Mitch grasped the chair, avoiding his assistance. He could have used a cane getting upstairs when his only elation was what he wasn't telling Dr. Dastin. He had just decided to finish his Ph.D.

"My 29th year was probably the worst of my life so far," I said after this long account and a bottle of wine in Mitch's disordered apartment. The coffee I was making let off its last steams in the kitchen. I found some milk to neutralize it. Mitch's night of numbers had caused me to imagine the years of a man's life in quipu knots that were based on a calendar of the stars. And then, I couldn't help but think of all the combinations of knots and how Mitch could compute their occurrences and probabilities with a computer program.

"We're so trained to look at the past," Mitch was saying. "Playing roulette makes you think that the past might not dictate the future. It's really good to see you again, Rosetta."

But I was grimacing. "Did you leave this milk out too? It's sour."

A CLOSE ONE

1

More stationary under snow, the cedar tree keeps Renata in a shadow behind the window. She watches for the young guy who is coming for her, anxious to see what kind of car he is driving. Having dreaded the new models with shark-like hoods and squinting headlights, Renata is relieved to see a nutmeg-orange vehicle with unassuming contours park at her house.

At the door, Renata's new acquaintance is taller than she remembered. She subtracts the years since a date made her stomach feel as if she were slipping on ice. And at once, she's glad that her husband isn't meeting the driving instructor she selected last week. At least he's a good ten years younger than her.

"I can call you Renata? And you call me Milo. It makes things easier in an exigency," the Duluth man says so professionally that he sounds suave. Renata doesn't think of Northern Minnesotan men as being suave.

She has to lower her eyes; the coruscating snow and sun have the force of a storm. When Milo hands her the car keys, they spatter until Renata is holding a rabbit's foot. She crunches around the car's chrome, discovering that it's a Sundance. Then she belts herself into the driver's seat for the first time in seven years.

"I had to take the written test twice," Renata warns Milo. "I wasn't expecting to take a drive in a computer."

The man beside her praises the new computerized test as he helps her locate the turn signal lever, so dainty in this decade's evolution that Renata only needs to flick it. Pulling up the emergency brake, starting the car, tamping the brake with her foot all happens without much thought. As the heat flares on, Renata gropes in her purse for her glasses.

She would rather not have the man beside her delineated even if she can't see the toll of holiday accidents that are undoubtedly on his brain. He must be very brave.

"I have lazy eye," Renata explains, seeing in the corner of her lazy eye a stuffed jacket. She careens from the curb in fresh snow that makes a clean slate of her path.

"Take a right at the next block." Milo's voice must be ritually calm. "Are your glasses required? We'll go by the stream and past the little Post Office. To the elementary school that's not in use."

Renata nods her tam-o-shanter pom pom back and forth. Her immediate elation, the casual cruising around of many years ago, makes her uneasy. The landscape is as special as a party, the trees nappy with frost and their twigs sprayed with an icy glitter.

Feeling empowered, Renata boasts to Milo that she doesn't have lazy limbs, that she is athletic. "But I usually do sports that give me a lot of space, like canoeing. When I take my little girl ice skating, I skid into people more than she does." Renata leads up to the matter because she can't help socializing with Milo.

She can't say yet what disillusioned the cheerful, courageous man she used to know. After the socializing. The look that begins to form another face. The first time she saw it was in a bumper car at a county fair. Her car revolving like something caught in the weatherman's storm center. He kept passing her with that look on his face.

"Is your little girl in school today?" Milo inquires.

"No. She's staying with a neighbor down the block," Renata replies, getting ready to be frank with Milo. If he's shooting the breeze, she's afraid that his words will freeze in the air. "I've had accidents in neighborhoods this quiet. It's not on my driving record. My insurance has paid out hundreds and hundreds of dollars."

Milo doesn't flinch for the near future. "But you're telling me that. I get all kinds of records. Do you think you have problems concentrating?"

The intrepid man leaps from the car, leaving Renata to concentrate while he sets up an obstacle course of orange cones on the school playground. Here, aggressive, self-propelled actions were apprehended and made base by towering, apocalyptic beings. The cones seem to be the noses of stupendous fallen snowmen.

"Let's see you weave around the cones," Milo says, adjusting his seatbelt.

"I think I was over-confident," Renata says, lining up the Sundance. "I rarely see a doctor. So I was careless about my eyesight." She careens towards the first cone, finding that she can actually keep talking. "My first car was a Gremlin. I thought it was the car."

A green Gremlin. Funny and grotesque to the couple in her car pool. Their engagement was a school legend. Both set up already. So sure of themselves it didn't matter who sat in front. What mattered was to get out of the Nicollet neighborhood. Not to have youth confused with the inner city poor. Overcast skies settled in the streets there.

"Now use your turn signal before each cone," Milo says.

Run that one down before he kills someone, he jeered. She added: that woman's looking for a way out with what she's got to give the world. I'm trying to concentrate. The nicest people. Their parties would have the nicest people. Her hand-done greeting cards of little people living in the pigeonholes of a roll top desk. Their huge possessions. Poor Renata can't draw a lake dock so you can tell what it is. Her third grade teacher had to tell the art teacher. She could draw a stick figure with an Al Capp rain cloud over her head.

"Next, we'll get the cones ready for parallel parking," soothes the kindest voice Renata has heard for awhile. And this man hasn't fathomed any glitch in her. She's probably the familiar route of the female to him.

"Let me do this again without my glasses on," Renata detains him. "I couldn't even find my glasses before my written test. So I went to an eye doctor for a new pair. Without my glasses on now, I can see the frost tips on the windshield. I had no idea I should be seeing better."

Without her glasses on, Renata doesn't feel so closed in and the male mist beside her seems optimistic. He doesn't interrupt her.

"The eye doctor said I have no depth perception, using one eye," Renata complains, the cones clear before her. "He said I don't estimate distance well."

Snow was blowing in her eyes. The eye doctor in a hurry to get to a dinner for ophthalmologists in Grand Marais. No, I'd rather not postpone. You have no depth perception at all. She was looking at a new instrument and it popped her in the eye. Muscle response so keen that she leapt up and left. Any optician in Minneapolis... But you see in only two dimensions, not three. A respectful oriental man fooled her with a different brand of the pop-gun.

"You got closer to the cones this time," Milo says with the fascination of a man who has discovered a woman's eccentricities.

With her glasses on again, Renata relearns the sequence of parallel parking, feeling that she is earning the small star rewards of the grade school. Then she glides in sporadic residential traffic, telling Milo, "If people want a ride, I've been asking if I can canoe them somewhere. I've been in races. I suppose I would have to have prescription goggles to correct my peripheral vision."

"Huh! Why not?" Milo said. "I like to cross-country ski in the woods for relaxation. This weekend, I'm renting resort cabins with a group of friends."

"It's hard to relax anywhere when you have children," Renata comments, rationalizing why these days, she and her husband often halt in conversation as if they are glancing at intersections.

Milo banters, "One of my friends would like to help design the transportation system of tomorrow. You purchase a computer card to borrow vehicles on a powered road. The traffic cops are in a computer precinct. An almost accident-proof system, he speculates. Kind of like bumper cars without the bumps."

Renata swills this optimism. It's like a time she once lived in, sunstruck with a man.

"Have any errands? People often need to stop at the grocery. My girlfriend didn't get oranges for the weekend. She said they were all dented at the supermarket. Let's see you park in some traffic," Milo prods.

She could do no wrong that winter. Parallel parking or suggesting the falafel restaurant. On a narrow needed street. An aura was around them. People would buy it if they could. Being in love is obvious as the brand-new. Like a display in a shop window. We have to hurry. She blurted out over her bean sprouts. Past people who could put their fingerprints on things. To the darkness and her macabre Gremlin. Hit-and-run. Her fender sticking into the street. That sinister shift as if the lighting had changed. When family life goes awry.

2

On her second outing with Milo, Renata is discussing skiing, how she goes downhill too. Then she finds she has driven to the crest of a hill with an angle of about forty-five degrees.

"The most important thing in Duluth is to have your brakes checked regularly," Milo states and then he alludes to a recent accident, a truck with faulty breaks hurtling towards Lake Superior. In the hospital, the driver denied any memory of his crash.

Renata inches down the roller coaster of a road system. Venturous residents daily skim from the hilltop to the downtown below.

"Pick a place for a downhill park," Milo coaxes as they sit at another intersection.

Her eyes on the rearview mirror and the prevalent Duluth pick-up truck approaching from behind, Renata ignores Milo. In her confusion, she puts on her turn signal. But then the pick-up truck blinks to turn too. Renata drives straight ahead which is down.

"It's only a little more than a bunny hill on the ski slopes," she says to bolster herself.

One day she was afraid. Of her husband. No, of the life they had set out on together. Stepped up like steep streets. They talked in code, coming and going from their new house. Nights were so perfectly tactile, they must be telepathic. And then he was one-upping his boss. A nice boss. Her husband's charm spent by the time he got home. So busy. The only person she could coordinate for tennis was the sender of the pigeonhole cards. Say no to part-time. He was like a predator after a hunk of money. Who needs time together for arguing about a second income? Back in her car, she bumped into another car at the bottom of the freeway ramp. Flumped into the grass and she was afraid.

Renata is gazing at Milo's understanding face, knowing that there is a code for completing a downhill park. Her wheels are jammed up against the curb yet she senses that she shouldn't pull up the emergency brake quite yet. It's been seven years.

"Turn the steering wheel all the way towards the curb," Milo reminds her, his tone commanding. "Do you believe in accidents? That things happen by accident?"

Renata is sitting on the slope, realizing that the thrills of this lesson have caused her to use Milo's arm as a support for her elbow.

Perhaps she divines that Milo was once seduced by one of his students, a divorcee, directly after Lesson Two.

In her discomfort, Renata replies, "I'd say that if there's an accident in our lives, then we are forced to admit it even if we don't remember how it happened."

Satisfied enough with this answer, Milo directs Renata onto a tassel of offshoot roads. They wind around the dominant slopes that comfort householders who have to think like pilots after breakfast. Relaxing, Renata knows her smile is coquettish.

Milo remarks, "I worry about people who put too much faith in fate." And then for some reason, he casually tells Renata how he met his girlfriend at Spirit Mountain, skiing. He gropes though, watching Renata, an active woman whose car traumas were in her wifehood. Even when he explains about curbs and gravity, he sees that Renata is insecure about parking a car up-hill.

She follows Milo's directions unswervingly, knowing that he will be happy as long as he believes that there is some randomness to his relationship. And then, without warning, she is hanging on the precipice of a sixty-degree hill.

"Are you trying to scare me, Milo?" Renata exclaims, trying to maintain her bond with her car seat. She hedges, "I should tell you how my grandmother never drove."

If Milo is meddling with Renata's emotions, he defends himself. "You'll probably want to avoid these streets but people stray onto them. I'd like to know about your grandmother when you can tell me."

Renata creeps down the alpine street, her foot hovering over the break as if she is an organist who has seen God, down, down to the downtown where a man honks at her at an intersection, her husband! Milo urges her to turn left, on level Superior Street going to East Duluth.

East Duluth when her grandfather died. About the time her mother (Renata, you're spilling again) stared at a dress display from their fabulously finned car and Renata had to yell at her. Crazy woman driver, a man yelled. Her only accident all these years. Grandma's yard used to be country. Snowshoeing wasn't for fun then. It wasn't just that her grandfather took her out on the Pike Lake ice and whirled her in contortions never known to woman. It was his rotten devotion. Like the horror films, real car accidents, that they showed at school. And

Grandpa banished Grandma from hearing Mae West jokes when his hunting friends were over. He was never anyone to talk to, was he?

"A woman driving was like smoking cigarettes in 1935," Milo laughs about her grandmother's driving lesson on Pike Lake.

"My worst accident happened because of glare ice," Renata informs Milo. "It wasn't because of my eyesight."

Seeing her arms stiffen, Milo airs one of his theories. "When people are in cars, they have to live in the present at all times."

A yellow light has turned red and they are waiting at an empty intersection. Renata turns to Milo and in their smiling is the realization that they are happy in the present.

"Have any errands? But you see, drivers can't be purely in the present," Milo qualifies his statement.

Renata's face has furrowed into a day's triptych that takes them to a snowy Shangri-la of houses, houses kept in a continual state of youth.

3

They are such a ritual now that Renata, afraid of Milo beeping the Sundance's horn, grabs her gear and heads to the garish Student Driver banner. Yet she has said that her husband should meet Milo.

"Ready for the freeway?" Milo asks.

"After the accident, I could drive anywhere in the city without getting on a freeway," Renata cautions. "My friends didn't like it."

"What happened to your Gremlin?" Milo wonders.

"Totaled. I wasn't hurt."

Milo doesn't press her for details because they are soon swinging up Central Avenue to the highway. The precise parallelograms of housing projects and the stilty porches mark slopes that might be re-defined in the spring. With the smoothness of a take-off, the Sundance rises from Lake Superior and mounts into the small-town atmosphere of lackluster businesses, cattail marshes, rural houses ensconced in evergreen, and beyond to the triumph of the mall.

"I see all the scenery on the bus," Renata says, her eyes fixed on the lanes in front of her.

Soaring on it. An ecstasy, putting things behind. And then the getaways dreamed about on a half-empty Duluth bus. The driver serene, formal, like a chauffeur. Milo has the temperament of a Hawaiian Island. They fished on a little island where the landmarks were a secret. Go there again? Stranded in a one-hotel town. The Rabbit's ignition gone. Furniture from the fifties, bashful with crocheted veiling. He thought it was funny. Those Chevrolet citizens, placid and apart as palm trees. Haven't gotten those Rabbit parts yet. And then the rescued disappeared off the face of the earth.

"Try to swerve into the left turn lane before the lights," the man at Renata's right says sharply. They are scudding under marble blue that seems leery about planetary adaptations. The pick-ups are teeming together, most drivers are pros at passing, the buses are non-negotiable. Too timid as yet to move with her blinker, Renata gets glances that make her feel as if she's flirting in church. Her blinker is so dainty that when she turns it off, it flips up and says she's going into the right lane. Still in the central lane at the lights, she looks away from the white wall of bus on her right. On the other side, drivers stare like aliens.

"That's why I haven't gotten on a freeway for so long. Because you can't get off until it says so," Renata explains when she is unfettered of traffic.

Milo buoys her with conversation about his sister, once a guard on a girl's basketball team, now hoping to become a highway patrolwoman. But while Renata has to turn around into another confrontation with the traffic, she realizes that Milo has never told her what his girlfriend does. She imagines that Milo can acquire a metallic male aura, making it easier for him to come and go. Stuck on the freeway, Renata considers how she didn't marry the man she knew. She married a life.

"At any time, my sister could be called to an accident site. Mostly for observation," Milo is saying.

The day of the accident. He was buffing his hair with a brush that fit in his hand. Where did he get it? Did he hear? About the plans to charge admission to city parks. Houses in Duluth are cheaper. She said it again, he replied to himself in the mirror. Loving her helped him to love himself first. They're putting street names on roads around lakes up there.

"It's not a race," Milo coaches. "It's got to do more with coordination and timing."

4

Milo made a reservation for a driving test, Renata's last lesson in the Sundance.

"I'm planning to buy a car," Renata explains to Milo. "My husband prefers a stick shift for the hills up here." Practicing for her test, she exaggerates every gesture in starting up the Sundance and entering traffic.

In her periphery, Milo is candid today. "Does your husband support your driving?"

Renata peers with Milo at other cars as if looking for her husband's hidden motives. At a vacant avenue, she replies, "Of course he wants me to drive like other people."

And Milo is being paid for moral support. Her husband was out of that. The day she stumbled in without a car. He looked at her as if she were a mirror with a third dimension. Wanting to make sure she was alright. She didn't have to go to the hospital. Persuaded him of that and the move.

"See that guy?"

Milo nods at a driver whose gaze says he doesn't feel like second-guessing a student. "I didn't prepare you for something. There are three people who give the test. A man who hasn't gone gray, a woman, and an older gray-haired man. The first two are positive but the older guy acts as if he knows about every reckless thing you've ever done. His bad mood is good for the teenagers, I guess."

"Milo, you could not possibly have prepared me for him," Renata replies.

They sit in the Sundance, stalling and talking until it is time for Renata to report for her test at the licensing center.

When Renata returns from her ordeal, Milo leaps up from a classroom chair. Consistent with her luck concerning vehicles, Renata has had the pessimistic examiner.

He speaks first, irascibly, as if he wants to keep putting things in the imperative. "She's passed. Seventy-two." He glares grimly at Milo. He must know about Milo's upholstered instruction.

Outside where Renata can be flabbergasted, Milo motions for her to drive again.

"I flunked parallel parking," she explains. "One thing wrong and he *is* unnerving. He took off all the points. That happened when I was sixteen. I got exactly the same score when I was sixteen! I wore my glasses both times."

As they head for East Duluth, Milo says, "Do you have any errands?"

"Yes, if you don't mind," Renata replies. "A ten-pound bag of flour and a ten-pound bag of potatoes. Does it bother you that people drive with low scores?"

Will it bother her husband? That day. Cold, gleaming, naked with spring. Didn't want to think about him in the metallic mirror. Driving home. Dreaming about going on west with 94W. Until mountain ranges were roadside rests. And then the chaste self-sufficient ranges. The hopeful indulgent rain. On Puget Sound, where her brother lived.

Renata has obtained her bulky essentials and she is about to start up the Sundance from a sidestreet near the grocery. But she has to deal with something crucial in the next few seconds. Milo is taking in the sight of her and she feels the closeness before kissing someone. Milo is so hopeful.

All at once, Renata is finished and she is sixteen-years-old. Milo is old enough to have learnt how after this moment, too many attempts are made to regain it.

There wasn't a clear freeway going west. There were cars, two, four, five splayed around the bend at the Mississippi. Across the sudden sheer ice. She had only a few moments. Not time to think about the unreality of death. Do not yank the wheel. Go with the ice until you get control.

They are savoring the Sundance's heat and Milo is confessing that one day, he opened up the newspaper to see that a former student of his was in an alcohol-related accident. He knew the teenager was as haphazard as a thunderbolt.

Reluctantly, Renata and Milo are saying goodbye and Renata, shaken but without any bodily trauma, is walking away from the Sundance towards the shadow of the cedar and the life that is one-way.

AN ELDERLY WOMAN AND AN ADOLESCENT

"Is the girl upstairs yours?"

The customer was hesitating from writing "Victorian House Antiques" in her checkbook. Lloyd had prepared Lil Butterstead for the banter that led to last-minute dickerings about price. Opals jiggled from the woman's ears and a gold bracelet girded her Bulova watch.

"A girl? They often stray from their mothers. Was she in the room with the doll schoolhouse or the room with the cradle?" Mrs. Butterstead humored the woman's reluctance to write a three-figure amount for an inlaid table. People had excused themselves from buying it after they saw the pegs for spools of thread in the table's drawer.

"She's wearing cut-off jeans with lace at the hem. They almost looked like bloomers," the woman dawdled.

"Hmmmm." Mrs. Butterstead noticed a girl who was familiar to her in a disturbing way. "The table, as I told you, was custom-made. People are so drawn to the mother-of-pearl inlay. You could easily have the pegs in the drawer sawed off. A little sanding and it's just for you." Lloyd would have detested such a suggestion. "A driver's license should be sufficient. My partners will be back from Chicago Monday if you need our help lifting it."

"That won't be necessary. My husband is over there. I guess he wants to buy some marbles."

He was solid as a cast iron safe. Her eyesight worsening because of diabetes, Mrs. Butterstead couldn't make Braille of the woman's embossed license number.

"I'm losing my marbles," Mrs. Butterstead said, ringing up the sum. "My husband knew where to get those marbles, the old milk glass ones," she explained. "He passed on this year and so did my marbles chum from childhood. But I can hold the door for you."

The gall of the woman, Mrs. Butterstead mused with a smile stuck on her face as the couple conveyed the table past the oak door. To insinuate that she would post a girl in the upstairs bedroom wearing something flimsy and resembling Victorian underwear! But this was the weekend when thefts might surpass the pay of a shop assistant.

If Adele, her marbles chum, had seen the stairwell wallpaper with the bleeding hearts, she would have been reminded of the back staircases of her childhood home. The banker's house.

But Adele's obituary was in the metro newspaper two months after her husband died. Because Lil Butterstead was following the traffic signals of her circulation now, she paused on the staircase to straighten a photograph. It was a prairie-scape like the environs of her hometown. And during the Depression, all cloud and loam. That was when Lloyd began creeping up the banker's back stairs like a cat burglar. Skillful pool player that he was, he had shown her how to set up mirrors in the turret area of the Victorian antique house.

From the turret, Mrs. Butterstead could already view the girl in the nice bedroom as she talked about the mirrors with a customer.

"The design on the border of this mirror makes me think of the temple-style banks they built early in the century. Before the Crash, of course. Yes, that's a lovely Maxfield Parrish print in the rustic bedroom."

After garden parties at the banker's house, Lil and Adele used to loll about on the lawn, their lemonade glasses on silver coasters.

"Oh yes, this commercial mirror would be wonderful for a lake place. Or a lodge. With the girl fishing out of it." But Mrs. Butterstead was watching the girl with the lace strips cross the hall from the nice bedroom and wander into the rustic bedroom.

Herding the customer into the rustic bedroom, Mrs. Butterstead let her examine the Maxfield Parrish print while she sidled near the girl. An heirloom embroidered teapot warmer had tempted the girl to look at the pricetag. Meanwhile, the customer postponed buying the Parrish print. Mrs. Butterstead assured her that husbands needed to be consulted.

"Are you looking for a gift?" she asked the girl.

There had to be many girls similar to this one: hair the gleaming brown of tea, its ends a crochet of curl; tea-colored eyes behind glasses; around a hundred pounds, maybe five feet, three inches; about fourteen-years-old. That would have been Adele's statistics then. Yet Mrs. Butterstead had forgotten the exact features of her face. All the metro obit told was Adele's age and the names of her survivors, her husband and five children.

The girl nodded and continued looking through the linens.

A woman in a tulip-red blouse had come in. "Since you're up here, could I get you to open this cabinet case? I'm wondering about this plate."

Mrs. Butterstead did have Braille for the keys in her pocket. "That's a series of plates called 'Life on the Western Prairies.' Royal Cornwall and very reasonable." The girl had her back to Mrs. Butterstead and she was working her way around to the applewood bookcase. She took out one of Mrs. Butterstead's favorites, a book on Buckingham Palace.

Mrs. Butterstead gabbed, "It's funny to think that when people began settling here, a boy named Tom Cotton was found in Queen Victoria's palace. He had hidden himself in her chimneys. He lived there a year, which explained some sooty sheets. Better to earn passage to American then, huh?"

The girl put the book back and like a piece of furniture on wheels, she slid around the room until Mrs. Butterstead was watching her in the fishpond mirror, descending the stairs.

"It is amazing, isn't it? That boy in Buckingham Palace. There were only a few items missing. Two inkstands, a sword, and a pair of trousers."

That afternoon, a thirteen-year-old girl named Lorna Samuelson was reading an article on family violence in the newspaper. *Children who watch violence are more likely to resort to it themselves,* she pondered as her father wrenched the front door open. His mood that week made him remote yet firm about rituals. He didn't need to repeat his request for Lorna to surrender the newspaper.

Lorna-just-like-her-father.

She watched her father skip over the home section, hurdle to the sports pages, and then return to the front page, what he did every day. Then he put down the newspaper and went to get a beer, daring anyone to take the newspaper from his chair.

Lorna didn't believe she was so dumb as monkey-see, monkey-do. She couldn't imagine herself doing what her parents did last year before vacation. They were going on vacation tomorrow morning and the argument had already started last night.

Lorna, her brother Skip, and her little sister Kelsey had eaten early, at 4:30, so her mother could clean out the refrigerator and get them ready for traveling. Her father had gotten off at three p.m. but he came home later than he'd promised. The early dinner pork chops, done in brown sugar sauce, were tarry when they were reheated. They stuck to her father's teeth, he complained.

He had run into his old friend Rando. "That's right, Randy. He's the one who could afford an architect to plan his log lake cabin." They could spend a few days there or at a campsite nearby if they all liked camping so much.

"You had hard liquor during your happy hour," Lorna's mother remarked. "Listen. We've got to move your mother's furniture to the basement. You said you'd have that done yesterday."

"You've varnished the pork chops," Lorna's father said.

They were eating early, Lorna's mother reminded him.

He thought she had her furniture refinishing class that day. She could hardly stand to miss it during vacation. It wasn't every day that he ran into Rando and today was happy hour.

That was the trouble with him. He might have called. But she supposed that he was acting like the Jolly Green Outdoors Guy again. If he was going to start behaving like someone who had never known a home like his mother's... Lorna's mother didn't say what she would do but her voice had some finish to it.

Home! If she would think of him for once! He wanted that walnut furniture sold right from the garage. She cooked for the children and planned her meals around her classes. Candied pork chops! Lucky her, he could eat camping provisions. She might have told him that she lived on salads before they got married.

Instead of packing up in her room, Lorna sat in the living room with Skip, playing Chinese checkers. From there, she could see the pork chop plummeting to the linoleum. At least it wasn't a china plate. Their retriever, Zappa, played hockey with it, enraging her mother.

As if he thought of her! Now she had to scrub the floor again! They'd come back to ants or worse!

Lorna's five-year-old sister Kelsey screamed. She wanted a marble but Skip held it tightly, his head turned towards the kitchen.

Now he had upset the children, Lorna's mother cried, coming into the living room to comfort Kelsey.

Lorna's father followed her. *The walnut furniture would make their living room look like a modular morgue.*

As if his mother's chairs would make him mournful, not the money that wasn't so solid. He shouldn't be using her as an excuse to act sick. This manic-macho stuff. Happy with Randy and who could like his downside at home?

Did he care? Lorna's father's hand rested on the glass plant stand. He had to demonstrate how the copper girders wobbled at its base, making its three round wedding cake tiers unsteady.

Lorna and Skip cleared out of the way. Kelsey crawled into the cubby of the living room desk. Lorna ran upstairs and got her new lavender tape deck from her room. She sat on the stairs, playing Blood and Roses at low volume, risking her father hearing it. He'd probably rail about the tape deck and throw it like the pork chop, calling it or the music junk. If tonight was like last year, he would be easier on her than her mother.

She couldn't sell the rattan furniture that had gotten them into debt! If it was time for new furniture, she made a mistake.

Lorna could see her father kicking at the couch leg to make his point. Then he fell back on the plant stand. Its glass disks toppled along with cascading baby's tears, hoya rope, and jade figurines. It all broke over the fireplace brick, the impact mixing with wails.

"Oh, you didn't want to move that?" Lorna's father wheedled in his alcohol voice. He swore about a marble being underfoot.

Lorna listened for the crunch of the refrigerator door and the wheeze of the screen door. Then she heard her mother on the telephone. She ran into the living room and stooped over the torrent of roots and leaves. Then she got the fireside broom and started sweeping the dirt towards the grate, only to find that the jade deer had lost an antler. Behind her, Skip picked up blunt pieces of glass.

"Get *away* from that glass. Has it cut your hand?" Lorna's mother was sitting near Kelsey, examining her with one hand on the phone. *No, they were alright and could come in the car. It was parked out front since they had furniture in their garage. He might have injured the youngest. Glass flying around. She wasn't sure. He would have liked to do that to her, yes, he wanted to hurt her.*

Lorna and Skip had to go upstairs and pack, she said.

At the landing window, Lorna saw her father at the backyard grill, already shaping a hamburger for it. She raced her mother, stuffing basics and visitor's clothing into her canvas camping satchel. With her woods tread, she decided to avoid the women's shelter. A motley group of women were always sitting on the porch there, not caring who saw them from the street. That's what her father said when they drove past.

Lorna was already downstairs when her mother came from Skip's bedroom on the first floor. As soon as her mother went upstairs, Lorna called, "I'm going to Brenda's house."

She was at the front door when she heard her mother call "Lorna!", not catching up with her, not stopping her. Sprinting away, Lorna took the avenue. Then she ran through the alleyways until she was across from Victorian House Antiques. She passed the benches with carved-out hearts and went in under the stained glass lintel.

"As I said, these are all Royal Cornwall 'Life on the Western Prairies' plates. The top one makes me think of Michelangelo – the boy and girl trying to touch hands as they ride horses. Something like that happened when I was a girl only the boy was on snowshoes and I wasn't so I sank. These plates can go separately."

Since Lloyd was gone, so many objects tempted Mrs. Butterstead with memories. What the plate evoked would not melt from her mind if she got as brittle as an icicle. As Mrs. Butterstead waited for the woman, gesturing for her friend now, she browsed the bedroom for shoplifted items.

Adele was a girl she could never catch up with, a girl in a white rabbit hood and trimmings.

She kept thinking that Adele's coat was white too, people wore so much white then. But it was Adele who wore the snowshoes that Lloyd carved and wove with rawhide.

Lloyd promised that the banker's daughter would walk on waves after a blizzard.

The scene seemed so bridal, Adele with her hands in a rabbit muff and the snowshoes lagging behind her like a train. Beforehand, Lloyd led Lil to the drifts, demonstrating to Adele's father how Lil became mired in the snow while he and his snowshoes stayed atop it. The banker peered at her, his sight much poorer than he knew, and then he paid Lloyd the precious few dollars for Adele's snowshoes.

Lloyd and Adele surmounted the banks of the stream on their snowshoes and then they tumbled onto the ice, sliding down the wide, sinuous aisle.

Mrs. Butterstead watched the two women knelling like bells over the Royal Cornwall plates. They both wore silk blouses and sported pointy haircuts. Gratified, she allowed a few minutes for an attachment. "I'll be in the hallway," she said.

In the banker's house, the scrolled mahogany cabinets with their bear-like bases awed Lloyd out of self-consciousness. Adele's mother set out two more lunch plates of Spode when the snowshoes were a success. Lil had been going over to Adele's to listen to the phonograph. She and

Lloyd were like two waifs in Queen Victoria's sloppy palace. But it was only a banker's house with back stairways.

Lil checked the nicer bedroom where the doll schoolhouse was set up. Most girls that age were fascinated with its thimble-sized bell and the marble-sized globe on the teacher's desk. Adele would have wanted it even though she had a fourteen-room doll's house. No, everything was there and on the white-painted vanity that her partners found. The crystal perfume bottles, the bead purse.

She felt uneasy lately with the things that had outlasted people. Especially those that reminded her of a day when the snow sparkled like Fostoria. She and Adele talking in Adele's bedroom about going to college and having splendid weddings. It all crashed so quickly.

"How are you with the plates?" Mrs. Butterstead asked the ladies in daffodil and tulip silk. "My husband would have liked them. He was quite a history buff. After the Depression, people couldn't afford college so easily. I'm still not clear about how President Reagan went."

"His ambiance makes him more appreciated," said the lady in daffodil. "I like this plate with the children on horses so much better than the others. But one plate seems so out-of-context."

"It's Royal Cornwall's combination of Laura Ingalls Wilder and Michelangelo," Lil said.

"We'll be back," said the woman in the tulip silk. "If she wants it at home, she'll be back tomorrow."

The sale of the snowshoes started the afternoons at Adele's, Mrs. Butterstead reminisced to herself as she opened a jewelry case for two college kids. The girl had to handle an antique enamel chatelaine.

The banker didn't know they were in his house unless she and Lloyd laughed on the back staircase. They could smell his cigar trail. Lloyd had been studying the phonograph cabinet in the study. And then he took an ax to the cabinet he was building, reducing it to firewood. He had to saw down trees for fuel, out in the woods earning hardly anything.

"Yes, there's time for you to see the upstairs before we close," Mrs. Butterstead said to the young couple. And she wanted to make sure that the candleholders were still in the bedrooms, Candlewick and the floral porcelain ones.

Since Lloyd was gone, Mrs. Butterstead liked closing up at the Victorian house. Tonight though, the used canopy bed frame upstairs bothered her. A jolt when her partners brought it in. She should remember such a bed as the perch of two Maxfield Parrish girls.

Lil and Adele giggling about bundling. That was a country custom of some German farm neighbors, the rumor went around the high school. The young man climbed into his fiance's bedroom to bundle, occupying her bed for a few hours. Adele had wondered, "Do you believe they kept their clothes on?" Lil sang a song because she didn't know how to answer her. Lil's parents said that only people in a sect bundled and people in sects had schisms.

But then one late afternoon, Lil walked in on Lloyd and Adele. Lloyd was leaving town the next day.

The Candlewick candleholders were still there.

But the canopy bed – there was a nude shoulder and Adele's silk slip on the floor. She stared at Lloyd under the counterpane, and at his bare foot beyond the edge of it. Lil sank downstairs, feeling much worse than she did when they were on snowshoes and she wasn't.

The young man's smile was discreet as he pointed out a vintage seed pearl necklace downstairs. He left his girlfriend in the antique house kitchen while he bought it.

Lloyd looked that way when Lil complained about their daughter co-habitating with her boyfriend. It was just as well that he kept sleeping with her, Lloyd argued. As usual, he was right. Ruth Ann wanted some old garters and an old cameo brooch for her wedding.

Locking up, Mrs. Butterstead still had a foreboding that someone had gone over her head in the painted lady house. She hadn't followed the girl downstairs, she thought as she examined the costume jewelry and the glass. The animal-covered milk glass dishes, dolphin and cat and squirrel, looked undisturbed. And the Hummel figurines.

Her partners would notice if anything were missing. If they thought Lil couldn't handle the store anymore, they would capitulate and hire a shop assistant. She was capable enough when Lloyd was alive. Her partners usually splurged at the Chicago antique show, bringing back odds and ends that required Lloyd's advice. She was still useful when it came to the wayward pieces of Depression glass.

From under a table of linens, Lorna heard the old woman humming and then muttering something about Adele.

"Adele knew the words. They had the phonograph."

The old woman thought she was alone. She didn't know that Lorna had loitered in the kitchen of the Victorian house, pretending to be interested in jugs that she might play in a band. When she heard the old cash register dinging at closing time, she eluded the old lady, slipped upstairs, and crawled under the table. If the old lady found her, she had some handkerchiefs that she could say dropped down. The tablecloth didn't quite hang to the floor but Lorna crouched against the wall.

She thought she might start sobbing when she saw the old woman's foam-heeled shoes doddering as if her feet were asleep. The old woman resembled a silver sugar bowl. Lorna couldn't imagine her doing anything without discussion.

There used to be an old man here, her husband. His hair was like pigeon feathers and he was as dignified as an old clock when he gave Lorna twists of hard candy, stopping her from petting china Chihuahuas. Lorna's mother brought the old man a bureau drawer that had become unhinged and then a chair that needed its seat rewoven. A few weeks ago, Lorna's mother talked the blue streak of a Friday afternoon with the old woman about the walnut furniture while Lorna wandered around the store.

When dusk shadows trudged the floor like watchmen, Lorna sat on the floor near the table, staring at objects that reminded her of her grandparents' house. The plate with a girl and a boy on horseback almost touching hands. A huge, hammer-armed chair that was all buttoned around. An old pitcher and jug like the one Lorna's grandmother got out when Lorna had a fever at her house. The framed old photograph of a woman wearing black. Porcelain doorknobs.

Since she had scared herself motionless under the table, Lorna felt as glum as the face in the old photograph. The woman seemed severe, staring at the beautiful picture of two girls sitting near some columns.

Lorna had whiled away the evening reading the book on Buckingham Palace. She'd found the part about a boy hiding there. And now she shivered as all the comforting objects disappeared into the dark. She might as well have gone to the women's shelter.

It happens about twice a year, she would be telling someone. *After Christmas and before we go on vacation and then sometimes in between. My dad gets drunk and starts picking out some object to bash up. He usually says it's because my mother made a poor purchase. But I think she sold my grandmother's plates because of him doing that. I guess he went to parties called bashes before I was born. His hair was long then. He broke a pottery vase because he said the cave drawings on it weren't any good. He dented a no-stick pan. Last summer he threw beer on some new drapes that my mother chose. It's scary and I usually run from the room. But so far he's like a fender bender and nobody gets hurt. He doesn't have fender benders; my mother does.*

Lorna is in the dark, her mother would say. *Look at her, playing vampire. He hasn't laid a hand on her.*

The women at the shelter would probably know that policemen had visited their house. When they warned her father, he swaggered back at them and said things like, "What I give in this house I can take away."

The unpredictable snoring sounds from the road kept Lorna going over and over what she knew. Even though she didn't want to go to the women's shelter, she might have to tomorrow.

My mother is always exaggerating, she might blurt out. *My father says she exaggerates every time she goes shopping. And then last summer, after the drapes, they were so lovey-dovey on vacation. Now my mom's gone back to school and my dad is mad because there's not as much money.*

I think my father treats my mother worse than he treats anyone. In our neighborhood, everyone says hi to him since he went around demonstrating how to recycle. He even gave a bash and showed people how to stomp on cans.

Somewhere downstairs, a clock called out the cusp of her usual night: cuckoo, cuckoo, cuckoo. Ten times. A nice dad turning villain. Though Lorna, being a camper, had more tolerance for unyielding surfaces than most girls, she became the bump in the night. Towards the kerosene glow of a streetlight, she budged along the floor on a small braid rug, staying near the bookcase. An old cradle was near the cabinet with the plates. But then she saw her own silhouette, what wasn't supposed to be there, in a hall mirror.

Lorna sat near the hall, looking at the room that was now in black and ghost. It reminded her of her grandmother's wake, all the old people on the walnut furniture. Lorna suddenly understood how guilt made people afraid of ghosts. Ghosts were from a time that was more prim, a time when people wore twilight clothing and grim expressions in photographs. She wouldn't like to know their opinions.

The shadows fluttered over the linens like fingers. *She didn't have to marry him! Look what's happened of her own free will. Ha!*

And that young body isn't being made to mind anyone, the darkness on a bentwood rocker would probably answer like an old woman at the wake. *It's true, there were bruises on my arm under the long sleeve. As if the men out here were all gentlemen!*

Stolidly the hammer-armed chair loomed out. *I sat across from a television and watched what all our work was for. Enough to tempt the bark off an oak tree. And then they get into a temper because it's all tantalizing.*

Lorna wanted to run howling down to the veranda of the Victorian house and along the street. But she was locked inside Victorian House Antiques and like a ghost, she had to avoid physical contact with anything solid. Unless she lit the candle on the bookshelf. Then she might see the picture of the two girls and the heavenly sky above them. Riffling in her satchel for matches, Lorna couldn't remember whether the wick on the candle was white or sooty.

The candle flame intensified the streetlight glow. She impetuously put it out. Then she saw that the clouds were threadbare outside and the moon was shining through the partially drawn lace curtains. The room seemed to have developed into shades of old photographs. Lorna felt more calm, as if she was looking at lens calibrations when the eye doctor switched them and asked "Better or worse?"

But out in the hall, she discerned what looked like a ghost, the ghost of the Victorian house. Nodding in silver and alabaster, it was coming from the room with the canopy bed and the doll schoolhouse. Holding her scream, Lorna saw that the ghost was like starlight. But the mirrors in the hallway were reflecting moonlight back and forth. There was a breeze and trees outside the windows, shifting the light. She looked from one mirror to the other, the girl fishing into the eerie light. She was the ghost, watching for another ghost until she was dreaming it. The hallway was a wishing well and words were being tossed into it.

Better or worse? Worse or better? Does she think it will get better or worse? Is it better to stay around for the worse? Or is it worse to expect better? Did she think she could help his worse get better? How much worse is her better getting? Who is getting the better of whom? If they get through lots of worse, can they expect better-than-ever? Who is whose better? Should they have said at first, "Has it ever been better? How worse can your worse get?" When they've never felt better, they can say they'll take the worse. Maybe it's better that way. Or was it worse?

The sunlight made its return with its strong statements, that it was the moonlight, the starlight, the real thing and better, the unreal dawn. And that this day would be better. In the morning wakefulness that insomniacs know, Lorna told herself that she would not spend another sleepless night in Victorian House Antiques. Pulling shafts of her hair into a barrette, looking into a mirror with roses and ribbons on its perimeters, Lorna could see another side of herself with her better eye.

She changed clothes, putting on what runaways are not often described as wearing – a summer shift. Made of liver-spotted cream cotton, it had a dropped waist and one casual ruffle. Considering a chamber pot, Lorna had to keep moving, dancing and driven as a sprite, until she found a blocked-off bathroom.

After the rooster-loud cash register became activated and Lorna heard a carousel of creaking, she emerged from under the linen table, feeling like a breathing object.

"There was a time a person could be a butterfingers with these glasses," Mrs. Butterstead commented as a girl in her twenties bought wineglasses with the name "Dionysus" on them. But she said it to another customer, one she meant to help with Depression glass. The younger woman, her purse a rumple of hemp, was in a hurry to have the Dionysus glasses. Mrs. Butterstead wrapped them as skimpily as the girl was dressed.

She furnished a history of the glasses. "My husband knew the proprietors of Dionysus so when the restaurant closed, they called me about their glassware. Collector's items for anyone in this area. But you know, they got these glasses for the breaking. Years ago, when they did as the Greeks did at Dionysus, my husband threw his wine glass at the hearth. He said it had a releasing effect. I couldn't do it."

Mrs. Butterstead was relieved that the young woman went away without socializing, her bracelets clanking as if they were made from an alloy of tin cans.

The woman who was asking about the Depression glass paused between the parlor and the dining room, looking upstairs as if she were assessing a rain cloud. "Is the girl upstairs yours?"

"What girl? No. She must be with a customer." Mrs. Butterstead hadn't seen a girl come in. But there was a starburst effect when the front door opened to the morning sun.

"She was standing at the case with the plates. I asked her about them," the woman said, heading towards the Depression glass in the parlor.

Watching the staircase from the parlor, Mrs. Butterstead said, "We were lucky to get plates with that celery dish and platter. It's called

Mayfair and it came out in 1933, I think. They're expensive but there's not much Depression glass in blue, you know."

Pneumonia blue, Lil thought. *At home, Lil ate on pink Depression glass. Adele had stopped eating in 1938, just after her father immured himself at his bank. And her mother, always wearing that fawn silk, gave a disgruntled former garden party guest a choice between their Spode china and their silver tea service. It was only a few months after Lloyd left. Adele's skin had the sheen of a fever and when Lloyd visited her in the spring, her body was blue and bosomless under the canopy of her bed.*

"Yes, the blue is so delicate. It makes a lovely table display," the customer said.

That was the last time Lloyd saw Adele.

The Mayfair plates were vein blue, the color Mrs. Butterstead looked for when she gave herself insulin shots. Plump after her pregnancy in 1946, she found out she had diabetes. Whenever Lil gained weight, she had to go back on the insulin. Lloyd handled her like Depression glass, put her on a shelf. He hated things that were tawdry, hated thinking about needles, made such a point of his own health, talking about the furniture he had to move when he dropped her off at the hospital. She knew at those times, when he hardly touched her, thoughtful as he was, he had deserted Adele.

"I can't promise any more of the Mayfair. But we might be getting more Depression glass in – pink and called Poppy. One of my partners has it stored. But you can't count on any pieces. They get separated from their sets, the way people did during the Depression. I had a friend who was well off one year, ill from malnutrition the next, and the next year, she had gone away to clean rooms in a boarding house that her relatives made of their home. If you need me, I'll be upstairs for a few minutes."

That was what it was about then, the lugging of a spiritless leg up the stairs when there didn't seem to be much point to it.

Lil avoided Adele too. There was that taint of retribution everywhere, and she was tending the vegetable garden that her parents made of their front lawn. People made jokes about Adele reading in her canopy bed when she couldn't go to college. Lil had to wonder if Jeanne spilled what Lil told her about Adele and Lloyd – Jeanne seemed so sensible. Adele wrote Lil postcards from the city, from the house of her poorer relations. "It's embarrassing. The people with eastern accents pronounce it 'bawding house.'"

The last time Lil wrote Adele, all she said was that the cabbages had a blight and she wouldn't grow them again.

Resting herself at the landing, Mrs. Butterstead looked for a girl's reflection in the hallway mirrors. Which bedroom was she in?

After Adele's last letter, she examined herself in her bedroom mirror. Adele had protested in her spired hand, "They made me marry." At nineteen, Lil could estimate the angle of Lloyd's rebound when he found out. And her compensation for showing Lloyd the words on the next page: "He has a job. He's very smart with automobiles. He can maintain them."

Mrs. Butterstead's face was still full and creamy, its wrinkles only hairline, like a cup of Spode. She couldn't help but notice as she looked for the girl in the mirrors and the doorways. In the rustic bedroom, the braid rug had pulled near the hall. It looked awful near the bleeding hearts wallpaper.

If a girl was upstairs alone, she was unusual not to have moved the tiny books and the dolls in the doll schoolhouse. Children wanted to shake the miniature bell and it had a tinny ding. But there wasn't a girl in the bedroom with the canopy bed.

There was only Lloyd's ax splitting a porch bench like the miniature benches in the schoolhouse, and his anger after he accused the banker of bartering his daughter. Lil married Lloyd anyway. The wedding was as pristine as Haviland china when there was only Depression glass for the reception.

But there was that girl now, looking like Adele in a low-waisted dress after the world had changed and Lloyd had sympathized about Ruth Ann's co-habitating with her boyfriend. The girl was looking piqued near the antique cradle.

Yes, Lil wanted everything that girl might have had then.

Mrs. Butterstead wandered around, straightening the linens. Then she was piqued, seeing a candle that had been lit and put out. They sold their candleholders with new candles in them.

"Just think, that cradle is probably from the Victorian period," Mrs. Butterstead said to the girl, the girl from last night, she was sure now. A familiar girl with those intent tea-colored eyes and hair like swirled tea on a sunny day.

"Of course the cradle is a Midwestern piece. A primitive, we call them in the antique business."

The girl peered at her through her glasses.

"Just think of it," Mrs. Butterstead said, relating her favorite story from Lloyd's history reading. "When Queen Victoria was reigning in England, there were two boys who hid themselves in Buckingham Palace. One sneaked through a window. Just imagine. He said he wanted to know the habits of people, that it would look well in a book! They put him on a prison treadmill and then they enlisted him in the English navy. He didn't have any stolen property on him. I think the story is in a book in this bookcase here."

The girl had gone pale as the lace-edged linens. But then she replied, "I could probably only afford an old book today. But I was wondering about this plate."

"Oh, that's Royal Cornwall china. It's their 'Life on the Western Prairie' series. They're not terribly expensive."

She examined the girl as the girl gazed from one plate to the next. Yes, she had seen her before. The girl might have been with the woman who sold the plates to her a few weeks ago.

"I might be back." The girl meandered towards the hallway and then Mrs. Butterstead could see her going to the stairs, her reflection in the art nouveau mirror and then the mirror with the girl fishing and then the floor mirror. It made Mrs. Butterfield feel more mystical than an antique dealer should be.

"Is your mother with you?" Mrs. Butterstead said, staying behind the girl who kept going on ahead of her. And then for a moment, they appraised each other as if they were both sensible of damages. Never having apprehended a shoplifter before, Mrs. Butterstead put her hand on the girl's arm. She clutched it, but because she didn't know what exactly to say, becoming confused she muttered "Adele."

The girl in the low-waisted shift fled like a specter to McDonald's where she ate an Egg McMuffin on her vacation savings. After that, she roamed until she came to a more well-to-do neighborhood. She felt like a free spirit, what her father was when he was young, her mother said. Lorna was lucky to run into a girl who chose her for squads at school. She was riding her bike and Lorna walked with her to her house and to the playhouse in her backyard. There, she told Renee about the old lady that she had escaped. She'd had to wear a dress to the antique house.

Out of the sun's interrogative glare, Lorna nearly fell asleep as Renee played with Kermit the Frog and Miss Piggy on her own stage. When Lorna didn't shriek at Miss Piggy toppling onto Kermit, she had to watch Miss Piggy pressing him and pinning him to the stage's proscenium. She had better be going. Renee's mother waved from a window above their hosta plants as Lorna ambled away, letting her basic sense of things direct her.

The sunshine was severe and Lorna, feeling horribly free, rambled on until she saw that her father's garage was open. The walnut furniture was no longer in the garage. Out of habit, she wandered into the kitchen where there were not only sandwich makings in the refrigerator but cans of pop for their vacation drive. The living room was clean and cool; the drapes were drawn. In the hallway, Lorna heard her parents' voices coming from their bedroom.

They heard her sandals on the stairs. None of this was ever going to happen again. As if they wanted to call those people with the playhouse. They would never be so hurting again, neither of them, none of them, ever. Lorna would never lie about where she was going and worry them again, would she? One bunking party at the women's shelter was enough for Lorna's mother. And her father was going to find someone besides an old bash buddy to talk with about his frustrations. They were planning to drive at dawn tomorrow morning. The last two days would be behind them.

STILL LIFE

She said there was a plum from their tree on the rosewood table.

There were three plums at the edge of the platter on the rosewood table. The light from the sideyard window wavered on the plums as if they added up to a jackpot. But they weren't replicas. The middle one was larger in size than the other two, probably from the farmer's market. Of the smaller two, one was striated puce-red, like a plaid with the sun's shaft across it. The other had more midnight blue in it. Flowering last spring, their plum tree looked like a straying girl in the twilight.

He didn't know which plum she had picked from the stepladder, the first plum of the season in the first season the tree had grown a plum. She had come from the farmer's market. She had compared plums.

He could see her, as he had seen her at the farmer's market last week when the sun shaved through the clouds. The day he first knew he was under the threat of the surgeon's knife.

She was placing squash, corn, apples, and plums on the platter, making things look good in the way people plump up pillows for the ailing. Nonchalantly, she could lose the platter at their house. He hadn't failed to remember it. A wedding present.

She was always keeping meals to wait for Mark, she said. She was on her way to the Sperry Lake Art Fair. Their schedules were topsy-turvy, as if they were planning picnics around severe weather warnings. Especially if she was going into the low pressure area, he didn't say. Dropping off that platter for what?

He invited them out to dinner then. The cirrus clouds, like shoestrings, made him restless. They could probably get it together, she said. And then Mark's answer later: Mara's gone somewhere with Bets for the day. I'll be over if she's not back in time.

They were too young to drift away from each other, he thought, telling his wife about dinner as she went out. Retirement happens like a shotgun honeymoon, he had said to Mark, screening his heart with Ray Bradbury. Even though he taught high school chemistry, Mark never came to him for advice.

And Mara gave him multiple-choice plums. How could he tell which was from his tree? The answer seemed to be in the day of the tree's planting.

His last child, Mark, whose derision always made him see litmus paper turning red, came home with a girl. There had been a long silence between them. He tried a school approach called mirroring with Mark. "Gees, that old apple tree came down so easily that I thought I was swinging a baseball bat, not an axe. Remember, you said it looked terminally miserable? You should have seen it after the last storm. But it left a gap."

"Let's plant a tree," Mara said too casually, with a teacher's certainty that she would get cooperation.

He wondered if the dark soil they tossed up would affect the color of the plums. He liked them on the violet side, the shade of one of the smaller plums on the platter. It wouldn't be as tangy as the crimson one. Of course, that also had to do with ripeness, he said to Mara. She brushed around Mark with the resilience of Artemisia. With her, Mark was alkaline. They were soon chatting about city life, what he had never tried.

Mara kept changing the subject, complimenting him about his backyard being so near the countryside. A suburban kid who became bubbly at seeing the kitchen pantry. They had a larder!

She must have seen the plum tree down the street and known that the backyard tree would germinate, he said. At that, she backed away and stood near the columbine. He and Mark clasped the tree, staking it, while she appraised its posture.

That night, Mark readily resumed their old game, Mark tossing realism at his professional optimism. He had his old glint of jealousy, the loner's, as they sat on the porch under the sky's plum-colored tarp. His sarcasm emerged like the teeth of corn under the green husk. But he began to see that if Mark was resentful, it didn't have to do with him anymore. There was someone else.

He didn't even show delight when the impish Mara asked to be dismissed. Her hands bobbed like yarrow, hiding her yawns during their discussion about organic foods. He could imagine her sweet sedition when she was in high school. Kids like that did improve. He laughed, recalling Mark's first date with a most exasperating sass. He had feared for his car.

How did he meet Mara? He went plum-wry, plum-sullen, his flavor much of the time. And there was the jealousy. Van knew her. He refinished a desk for her. And then she needed refinishing, he thought Mark mumbled. But he would rather ask heat lightning to repeat itself.

Van used to be a buffer between them, being one of the changeling children who asked him for advice. Van was a day of promise that could turn inclement tomorrow. He probably grew the squash in front of him, a handsome squash, green seeping down it like drizzle. He had a handsome face to protect in a catcher's mask.

Mark was in his tight-teethed slouch after Mara went inside that night. Only his resentment had settled on Van. Van had come over for the father-son ever since they were kids.

Van's father was still the local bogeyman, ever since he had knocked himself out, setting up a pumpkin shell shelter and sandbox at a nearby park. All the trappings supplied by his hardware store. What a memorial after he died, what a monument, to be said to revisit a park pumpkin shell at night, invisible except for a rope, a monkey wrench, and a hammer. And there he kept them very well.

Van had come back to live in an old family farmhouse outside of town, poverty-proof, a hand at the hardware store, an itinerant art teacher in county schools.

Two of the plums on the platter could be from *his* tree.

Moving the plums, he could verify only that the platter was from his son's wedding. His youngest son, come back as the weatherman. The platter was an extravaganza, a carved buck's head with its antlers stretching to apples at the border. A card sat on it after the wedding. Letitia. Mara probably brought it up from her basement, like a tumor.

The late light arched across the plums on the platter, as if consecrating them. He thought that about the sun's sudden glance at the farmer's market a week ago Saturday, the Saturday after the first week of school. It was as if the food had raised the folks there to be part of the land, ephemeral as the harvest, like fairy legends. The modern rustics made risks at an illogical level to grow the glimmering green corn, the mosaic squash, the apples that had the smatter of baseballs in the air, the plums with their twinges of twilight.

Mist was being distilled above the market that morning. He was indistinguishable from it in his gray raincoat and golf hat. He hardly felt visible as the school year started. He unsnarled a forefinger onto an apple, feeling the blood rise to his fingernail. The day after the doctor sent him for the tests that weren't back yet. He was afraid of picking out homegrown corn with rot in it. And of going to the grocery store for produce sprayed with compounds that could latch onto his weakening tissues.

The voices of the growers braced him. They were jocular with as much of a hard sell as they mustered, familiar but not saying his name. The grown version of local kids who saw school as subsistence learning, they had the conviction that they would get by. A vanishing breed.

And then light streamed into the marketplace, the glimpse that remembered the county's last century. The display seemed to be as much for idle appreciation as a platter of fruit and vegetables on a table not far from a microwave.

And that's about what he saw: a booth across the market with carrots glowing like candles and squash like the one in front of him. Van was juggling plums behind it, moving to encircle his arms around Mara, juggling the plums with her body as obstacle. A shot for a television commercial before the weather report. He thought he was forever numbed to Shiva-like arms reaching around in hallways. As if she were the farmer's wife, Mara stood behind the booth while Van stretched supine on the grass, still juggling.

More than once, he had cast a teacher with a studio style into the rags of his bachelor relationships. The new teachers had troubles already. But Mara knew Van.

He went away, empty-handed, unrecognized. He passed Mrs. Cuppner, once on a citizen's committee for choosing sex education curriculum. Years ago, she mentioned that his students said he seated the best-looking, mini-skirted girls in the front row of his classes. He said that he hadn't noticed. He put girls who talked too much in the front row. He was accustomed to student tomfoolery, could smell that a piece of prank rubber vomit was not a case of the flu. Kids didn't leave toilets on his doorstep as they did to English teachers with widow's peaks.

His hair turned prematurely white, he had a comfortable rapport with students. He used to feel like the school Socrates. Theirs was a county seat that still thrived from industry and a reputable hospital. He was known for his droll retort and his accessibility. He wore bow ties and western medallion neckpieces with light informal jackets that rumpled like his lab coat.

No one seemed to know him now. He was ring-around-the-head bald, an old man in a raincoat, gaping, leering. When he walked around town, he felt like a harmless but worrisome Mr. Hyde.

From a bench on the courthouse square, he asked a young lawyer what he thought about the DNA of a hair matching that of three other people besides a suspect. If there's other proof, he wouldn't worry, he said. But what bothered him were the bald suspects.

At the hardware store, he informed a young woman that microwaving a mother's milk destroyed the lysozymes that killed bacteria. She hoisted the microwave she was considering and carried it to the cashier's counter.

At the golf course, he asked a young man if he wanted to buy a new car when right now, they were developing syngas from the sun. I'm on the green in five minutes, he yelled.

He was disappearing into the ultraviolet range of life. For his family, he still materialized.

Smug plums. He couldn't tell which were his. People grafted marriages, moves, new jobs as swiftly as chemical reactions these days. A teacher's kid, people suspected, was like store-bought fruit set out with its rotten parts hidden. Mistrusting Mara reminded him of William Tell aiming an arrow at an apple on his son's head. He could lose his son if the town talked.

Controlling, subduing, channeling had been the activities of his life. And Mark's philosophy, ever since he began looking out windows, was naturalistic. With a meteorologist's logic, his son would prepare for what wouldn't answer to him. He could pack up without compromise and take a fifty-mile an hour wind to another job.

His youngest. When he prepared people, they disappeared. He wanted to stake Mark down. He could be still.

Why did artists call the harvest samples that appeared on platters "still life"? The squash was disconnected from the vine, the corn shorn at the stalk, the plums severed, the cherry wood embalmed in stain. He was the still life, a person that the artists hadn't made visible.

He was rocking near a platter of produce after floods of teenagers partied through the last rites of the high school. He went with them on their senior trip to the city, trips chaperoned with Miss Sheehan: I don't know what I'm going to do; I don't know if I'll get in; I don't know where to go; I don't know if I can pay for it; I don't know what will happen.

He was ready to go in his bone-white suit. He would write a prescriptive note: *I have gone on to the restaurant without you. Your dinner is in the refrigerator. Just put it in the oven for an hour or two.*

He hoped Mara was coming. With the squash, he went to the kitchen pantry and picked out a knife. The light of the day was diminished, older. He could stuff the squash with the sliced apples, corn from the cob, maybe a question of plum, dab butter and brown sugar, a little white wine on it all.

For himself, he would rather prepare a cup of poison than come under the knife. Chemistry is chockful of solutions for the future, he used to say. Results from lab tests, exploratories, treatments.

It seemed like corruption to him now. And the girls with the good legs were seated in the front row. Fishnet stockings, windowpane pantyhose, flowers blooming in lace on calves. Before Mrs. Cuppner's admonition, he had dared to lean a hand on a girl's desk, lecturing. The desk could tilt, and he pretended to be agog at a girl's dress drooping. It delighted the boys. Nothing much more, not even with Miss Sheehan after she had the custodian sprinkle sawdust on the prank vomit before sweeping it up. She didn't want to look at it later, a Halloween acquisition from a novelty shop.

He could play hooky, cut the doctor's lecture, drive up and down Main Street, chew gum, pluck at women's clothing, set up a few minor explosions, concoct his own cup.

The knife was on the still, lifeless squash when he heard his wife's sharp, slicing voice.

"Clayton, are you in the kitchen?"

She could see his bone-white suit now though her eyesight was dimming.

"There was a downpour at the art fair so we got on the road late. Mark and Mara are waiting in their jeep. Do you still want to go out to dinner? Mark says the rain will be here tonight."

He put down the knife, then put it away. "I hadn't thought of you all this time. Going to the art fair with Mara. I thought you were at their house, waiting with Mark. After whatever you did with your afternoon."

"I said I was going with Mara this morning, Clayton. What are you doing with that squash?"

"I thought I'd open it up and see how it looks inside." He put the squash back on the platter. "Look at these plums. One of them is ours. I can't tell which."

"From our tree?" his wife said.

"Do you remember this platter?"

"Didn't Mara's friend Letty buy it from Van? I was admiring it and she said it was gathering dust. Clayton, are you coming? We lost Bets to Van's booth at the art fair. He had some lovely stained antiques, his hardware sculptures, and then some sculptures that seemed a corruption of driftwood to me. But a watercolor was interesting, a still life. He painted abstract light figures along with the bowl and fruit."

He would be still. He would have to trust his young, the way they trusted the doctor. If he prepared people, if he prepared himself. At least his wife still followed his directions. Overshoes, raincoat, golf hat.

GOOD OLD GUS

As if he had fled to a cave, Sy was sitting above it all now. The mixed smoke in the room obscured the recent past. Already it was in his mind's museum: the avalanche of asphalt; sewage pipes showing like innards along ripped roads. A mess he left.

The woozy whining in the smoke was genuine. "We had just moved to Duluth. Everything was in upheaval, I thought. There was a storm in the night, but I slept through most of it. My mother and I couldn't drive downtown. The streets had caved in. It looked as if an earthquake hit."

At least she wasn't insipid, prodding him with fill-in-the-blank questions. The attempts to connect at college parties. Wasn't trying to know somebody. No wonder it was sociable to sit without speaking, to be laconic with a crowd getting wise, the mouth not becoming a lesion, to sit high. It was 1972.

"The storm wasn't a bad one," she went on. "I didn't hear torrents of rain. Just a thunderstorm."

She wanted an accounting from someone who was in Duluth when the streets washed down towards the lake. She looked as if something else had crumbled.

"Steep streets and an overloaded old sewer system," Sy said. He dredged at his cigarette and blew disillusionment around the dorm room. Through the smoke, lamps and candles gleamed like wall torches; the bead screens dripped like stalactites. She didn't know Duluth, wasn't from there. Most of the private college's occupants came from well-off homes in functioning communities. Embarrassing to flounder around about Duluth's prosperity being in the past and how the iron mines in the area were being depleted. A city literally going downhill. She should know that. He should ask her about herself.

His roommate Gus came to the rescue. Good old Gus.

"Wow, I was there. Sy and I were going to the Boundary Waters to canoe before school. Gees, I freaked out!"

Sy could spurt out smoke now. Embarrassing sometimes too was Gus, a fool to be so trusting and trustworthy. But his parents were rich and he had a permit for his car. Sy's disgust at the disaster abated when he watched Gus hang his head from his car window like a big pup. Sy's house was above the wrecked streets. Gus's long hair flapped around like an Indian's in the Boundary Waters. Gus, from New York.

People asked Gus, "Why did you come here for school?" They didn't say what was on their minds: *You're dumb, aren't you, and think you'll get into medical school easier here.* Gus claimed he wasn't premed, that he selected Minnesota because of the lakes.

Gus's concern for Duluth seemed patronizing as Sy urged him to drive away that day. There was nothing to do but leave. Gus had to park on a hill and look down at the landslide. The avenue bearing towards Lake Superior looked like a dried up river ravine with rubbish in the shallow places. Gus maundered, imposing his boyhood bad-trip dreams on the debacle. He wanted to walk downhill to see how the gutter went from warps to cracks to wreckage. Sy asked him how often he drove into New York City. He didn't have to behave like a city councilman.

Really, Gus acted like a kid at the movies, catatonic with the popcorn. Sy stewed over spending days in the wilderness with him. He handed Gus a camera so he could snap out of his trance. In the Boundary Waters, Gus was fine. He could carry the canoe himself; he even jaunted with it like a circus bear in the forest.

And now he was telling his psychological fears to this Nola person.

"From the hilltop, I could see how the sewage water unloaded into those streets with the rainwater. When I was a kid, I had recurring nightmares about rising water. Somehow I had to get through it to a slimy basement faucet in our old house. It turned into a phobia. I distrusted toilets. This was reality though."

"Gees, Gus," Sy said and passed him a joint.

Nola said, "It really made me wonder, moving to a national disaster area."

From floor pillows, crowded beds, and a hammock swing, this conversation was being attended. Snickers sounded between swigs from a leather winebag and subtle eye-smiles shot around the room. As if Gus had introduced people.

To judge that his fellow inmates at school were devoid of humanitarian concern was unfair on a weekend night. Especially after they had wearied their minds all week. Someone might have asked Nola where she moved from. Sy might have mentioned that Duluth was having trouble paying its plumbing bills. Nobody dared to break a party taboo and ask Nola what her father did. Some were probably noting Gus's phobia and thinking about ways to seal the shower drain.

"What a relief to go to the Boundary Waters. I couldn't have showered," Gus barreled on. "It always seemed wrong to me, all that water going down the drain from showers. When everywhere you looked, the water was getting polluted."

"Gus was absorbed with the subject of septics and didn't like getting gussied up," laughed Tim within his ferny hair. One of those honestly selfish products of the status quo, a skeptic if anyone idled in idealism.

"I still can't comprehend what happened in Duluth." Nola looked around Gus at Sy, in appeal.

Sy could speak without emotion. "The streets were due for repair. There aren't many cities with Duluth's hills. San Francisco. I'd rather worry about rains than earthquakes."

"The street upkeep must be stupendous." Gus cut in like a canoe paddler at the stern. "The snow melting down every winter. Maybe they'll make those hills more drivable. Wow. Some of those streets are like ski jumps."

The room's tenant then spoke from the upholstered chair he smuggled in. Since freshman year, he had emerged as a person de resistance. Richard's reserve was muscular though his arguments wouldn't be expressed physically. When he flared, his eyes filled in with blue and seemed to travel like a laser beam. He could handle being called the Prophet after he read Nietzsche and Castaneda. He liked people who wanted to get above their college existences, the herd scuttling to the cafeteria, to class. He knew they felt like idiots of convention. Then he often sat like an intractable mailbox where a person regretted a letter.

Actually, it was his voice that was like a laser. It was pleasant, singling out a person. "Duluth sounds like the travesty of so many people getting on in a small way. They treat anyone with awareness as if they're a fortuneteller. While consuming supplies and competing in a petty way for places. Avoiding any power that might prolong what doesn't last. They built mansions that the next generation can't afford."

He was elevating everyone in the room from being the average person, relieving them from the go-getter, from college claustrophobia. His beam was on Nola now. She seemed to have attained the telepathy that the sons of the silent majority used.

2

But Nola felt that Richard was the typical egotist, behaving as if his illuminations needed a patent.

She lived under Sy and Gus that year, on the female floor. The drifting Moody Blues music that put her in a stupor was Sy's, she found out. The brocade bedspread and the horsehair cushion were Sy's. So was the tapestry with cigar-smoking terriers around a poker table. The spider plant, gargantuan as a chandelier, was Sy's. And the lamp with the wizened wind face was Sy's.

The invitation to swill in Sy's taste was Gus's.

They had come from the study lounge where people were obstreperous near the piano. Nola was looking at Gus's side of the room from her perch on Sy's bed. Gus sat slouched on a vinyl dorm chair. His bedspread was utilitarian and jutted like a tarp over the end of his bed. The picture of a mermaid with breasts not unlike fish, opaline gouramis in the tank, was Gus's. The musty terrarium for turtles was Gus's. And the wall map with lakes and doodled routings was Gus's.

With the horsehair cushion at her back, Nola stretched her jeans on Sy's bed. She had to concentrate for a quiz the next morning. Lately, she had been glad to get away from Gus, glad to get to class. For all his floppy clothing and long hair, Gus was bent on the conventional. She had already rebuffed him about a Friday night concert. She had gone to her dorm hungry to keep Gus from accompanying her to the cafeteria.

If Gus wanted to resituate his body, Nola would give Sy a wave of exasperation. Actually, Nola was adding to the little she knew about Sy. When he happened on her, he was like a refreshing mist and she liked his wildness, the way his eyes sprang at her and then around her. Mildly muscled, he could look ascetic from whatever was eating at him. Anger or a secret anguish or even envy of Gus?

"What are you doing?" Nola demanded as Gus got up.

"I thought I'd put on the Moody Blues. OK with you?"

"OK. What's the name of that album?" She should know.

"Every Good Boy Deserves Favor."

Was that a reproof? This year, alienation gave Nola the pangs of an ulcer. And Gus was quick to supply a sudden necessity. Sy probably reflected on this too. Somewhere Gus had snapped up a safety pin after her bookbag strap ripped, probably from his ramshackle clothing. He had been supplying her with coffee in the dorm lounge. She was streaking sentences with his sunny highlighter seconds after hers ran dry.

Finishing up Herman Hesse's *The Steppenwolf* while the Moody Blues made an evanescence like spring clouds, Nola felt as if she were at the edge of campus, where she was last night. Pairs of students were on the tidy turf, pondering utopia and the lights switching on along the avenues of faculty housing. The sky was luminous as a negligee.

Nola was supposed to declare her major and meander the campus with a man if she wanted out from the herd. The sciences, society said. Her grades suggested it too. Simple like Gus.

But it wasn't. She didn't know where the doors really lead anymore than the Steppenwolf knew the theatre of mirrors.

Baby boomers stood in hallways, choosing from a list of possible professions. They seized on some penchant from childhood such as dispensing tablets of candy from a paper strip. And while they listened to people of lucky serendipity, chanting and mystically hovering in a twilight where a person needed their true self.

If she stops to take stock, without destiny, indefinite, Nola sees the shine of chalk on a blackboard. God knew. Music is an arrangement of cloud that veils an unearthly, unanswering silence. The college, filled with students who feel themselves to be penniless, is a stately establishment elevated from the plain. And while the turmoil of a great lake beats on, Duluth can turn to debris. Because it was secretly in decay. Where her father, having left the wolf of his barbiturates behind, was about to start a new pharmacist position. And where her mother, aghast at the streets, looked for a new nursing position and a church for praying against a relapse.

Nola lets women into her dorm room even though she is declaring that she doesn't think she can believe in God. Declare yourself, urge the professors who own black gowns with elegant chevrons. One by one, the women have declared themselves. Many have read Sartre and Camus in religion class. They have recoiled from Bible talks with a woman who seems to have a crush on Christ. And when Nola declares the obstacle of her choosing, that she can't believe in God, she sees that they feel sorry for her. Secretly.

"But can you say that for sure?" Her roommate is agile at asking people about themselves and at picking her way into cliques. Egotists have performed soliloquies for her. Yet this subject repulses these women back to the blonde-slabbed buildings that haven't caved in.

"Nola, have you decided what you're going to do..."

"Gus, I'm trying to decide whether I believe in God or not."

Nola knew that with Gus, this was an exit from intimacy, from making her declare her major or her plans for spring break. She was waiting for Sy to come in. Unwittingly she had registered for admittance into Sy's crowd. She had cloyed Gus on another existential evening. He wanted her to come to a party.

3

Nola was sitting on Richard's hammock, touching shoulders with Sy. Although she would rather face him than Richard reading Nietzsche, Sy was giving Richard all his attention.

"The small man recurs eternally! Naked I had once seen both, the greatest man and the smallest man: all-too-similar to each other, even the greatest all-too-human." Speaking like a professor with insomnia, Richard resonated beyond the tension line in his cheekbone.

Nola withstood this, having read some of the Nietzsche. The German philosopher seemed to be a foil at God's deathbed, having possession of an altered will. "God is dead," what *Time* magazine declared on its cover so many years later, made Nietszche seem like a prophet. She didn't like Nietzsche's contempt for the peon. It made her feel as if the milkman weren't coming anymore. But Nietzsche had called marriage a long conversation. Its preliminary might be this foggy physical meditation with Sy. Of course, Gus was sitting on her other side. He had been remarking on the long necks of giraffes and ostriches, making irrelevant points about small animals and great animals.

When Gus hid his head like an ostrich, Nola wondered, "Didn't the Nazis use Nietzsche to found their philosophy, Richard?"

Richard gazed at her with his gaslight eyes. "They misconstrued him, as Einstein was misused then. You must have missed the part where he hopes to rejoice with the Jews."

"But what does he mean by superfluous people?" Nola plunked her palms on her thighs as if she were going to play patty cake. She didn't understand how Richard could be so serious about this.

"Well, we're baby boomers and we know we're superfluous. Why do people come to this college? To rise above small people, to get themselves a little life. Nietzsche tries to define what is essential, to shake people out of smallmindedness."

"But don't you think many people do the best they can? And that every good boy deserves favor?" Nola was reminding them that "Nights in White Satin" was playing on the stereo.

Sy put his arm around Nola and patted Gus's head. Then Sy's eyes glinted from his profile. "People try and try and then they get snagged into one of society's schemes. They feel small and resent it," he said.

"But what if you happened upon this guy in a cave or a hut in the boonies? What would you think if you met him?" Nola wanted them to see the twilight of the music, not this philosophy. She craved for Sy to see the twilight outside with her, beeches redolent with catkins, redbuds along the manmade planes of the campus. Past the lawns, the unkempt epicurean lanes were filling up with loosestrife and cinquefoil. Fields were beyond, combed by nobodies.

Richard replied, "I think I'd feel his inner power. Like the Indian's presence in Casteneda's *Tales of Power*. I might see him wearing a suit in the city one day. Seeing him in a recluse's rooms, I'd know he had chosen."

Yet Nola could only envision Richard slouched in a certain echelon. He maintained his disillusioned air with a classmate of Nola's. The homemade chain cardigan she wore was probably like one her mother wore to church circle. After whispering with Richard, she ducked behind Nola and murmured, "C'mon. He wants us to leave."

Gus's too-new tennies creaked behind them. He loitered at Nola's door, his shirt like a collapsed awning. "It's not that they don't like you, Nola. They're dropping acid."

Nola was usually spontaneous with Gus. "I won't say 'More power to them.' Gus, Nietzsche really put me behind on a psych paper."

Buds seemed to be opening inside Nola and the sensation, painful in its unclenching, kept her awake. Being transplanted, she hadn't thought that further growth would be like the budding of the desperate backyard lilac. Nola tossed, hearing movements above her. She fumbled at her dresser for her sneaked bottle of Librium. Her finger as cold as her father's metal phalange, she extracted a capsule that was supposed to be for exam time only.

A few hours of sleep later, she was sitting on the window seat. The blaze of daybreak didn't perturb her roommate's slumber. Feeling languid from the tranquillizer, Nola dressed and meandered outside. As if a guard would sight the foe, aloneness, she dashed on under the redbuds. It was a thing of happiness, being superfluous, petal-possible, bathed in the morning light. There, under a beech tree, Sy and Richard were slouching on the grass, watching the sun rise. Richard got up. He was sturdy under the dripping tree, confident in a chesty, debauched way, how her father looked sometimes. His brown hair looked as if it had wood grain in its uncombed waves. The blue of his eyes was subdued in the strong dawn light. As he apprehended her, his height made it possible for him to glance down and then kiss her inconspicuously, which he did.

Gus was driving her through farmland that was impudent with fertilizer. Yet it calmed Nola more than the Librium she had swallowed before her Friday exam.

At lunch, across the cafeteria table, she heard Sy saying something about a Sunday drive. She rhapsodized about the countryside and Gus made the gesture. But Sy didn't join them in Gus's car.

"Boy, I was glad to get away," Gus said, his hair splaying into sheaves at the open window. "Sy's grandparents were in my room. It's their Sunday drive, visiting Sy."

"And they'd like to shear your hair." Nola's chagrin could only supply the short answer.

Twenty minutes from her hometown, she just wanted to daydream in the dull lecture of the land. The rank air had the lethargic effect of incense. As it imploded to her core, where Gus couldn't reach her, they passed a familiar diagonal-slatted fence behind which horses were kept. They were approaching town. Nola wanted to slump down in the car but instead, she fastened a peasant scarf in a headband around her head.

"Better slow down," she directed the big city boy. "Main Street is a speed trap even though it looks sleepy as Sunday. But they let the drug store stay open. There, with the old-fashioned awning. No, there's no soda counter anymore, just a bored pharmacist. Those girls in hooded sweatshirts are going to weigh themselves on the scale inside and accept their fortunes. If it looks bad, they'll act as if they have a backache and buy aspirin that, mixed with coke, rarely makes them high."

Nola didn't tell Gus that a man could crumble in such a town where the rutting of the young people, the tight lattice of the adults, the factory whistle, and the carapaced farmers chugging in for arthritis preparations made a person go punchy. There were adults who behaved the way students did when they stayed up all night, reviewing the same information over and over. Especially if a person was planted with the permanence of the littering peony bushes, furnished by speeders for the courthouse and bandshell lawns. Such a person is supposed to become bovine in temperament, her father used to say. The morning after someone called him in the middle of the night, needing heart medication. And then he needed his special blend of barbiturates. Who knew? Her mother wondered after she was relieved of handing out drugs at the hospital where she was an RN. The same week that Nola's father went out of town to purge his system.

Directing Gus along the avenues where wrap-around porches provided a full view of a block, turn here, take the curve there, tears lurked under Nola's eyelashes. She wiped them at the window, pointing out her old house because she liked the lavender stones on the lower story.

The peaceful prairie flatness had a kind of sanity, she said to Gus and feeling grateful. Streets didn't crumble in towns like that.

4

After Gus returned from his June canoe trip with Sy, calling Nola was a small worry.

During the trip, he imagined that she was like the unspoiled Boundary Waters, his reason for hanging out in Minnesota. She was not habitable, it seemed, and her wariness piqued him the way sounds did in the northern woods. He couldn't find any trail, talking with her, and too often, she gave him the brush off. Driving back to Duluth, Gus had to restrain himself from seeking Sy's go-ahead.

But then, the news flash came on about the entire water supply of Duluth being tainted with asbestos tailings from the mines. Gus couldn't believe how every time he visited Duluth, it was like going into New York City. And Sy had grown up drinking that water. He absorbed some of Sy's shock, couldn't help gasping at him as if he had been mugged and robbed. His health. The asbestos might cause cancer like cigarette smoke or smog. But without any warning. After Sy's initial outrage, he went as cool as ever, lit a cigarette, and began talking about Nietzsche's *Twilight of the Idols*.

At a gas station, Gus found out about a farmer who sold bottled spring water to resorts. When they drove into the city calamity, they were armed. At Sy's, Gus felt as if he had entered a house where the family just learned about the death of a person he didn't know. Sy tacked off into his moody solitude. So Gus took off for camping supplies that would last until New York, some of which might be at the drug store where Nola's father worked. Everyone he saw was in the glum limbo of a hospital waiting room. And the drug store was almost out of bottled water.

When he called Nola, she was working her way through a case of Dr. Pepper pop, as she called it. She kept restraining herself at the water tap as if it were a bad habit, she said.

"Two months of asbestos water can't have hurt me. I was thinking of you and Sy at my new waitress job. We had a flood of business, mostly liquid."

She wanted to go driving for another load of spring water. Sometimes Gus suspected that Nola might be as outdoorsy as him. She was scornful about the concerts and movies pandered at school. It was *him*, he thought, and then she exchanged confidences as if they had come to a clearing in the woods. But she bolted off to the lair of her night.

Nola couldn't stop talking about how Sy had imbibed asbestos all those years. Sy looked too ascetic to her; his skin was like fog. It was bad enough, she bitched beyond her distress, Richard and his acid trips.

"He doesn't suffer from fatigue. He seemed healthy enough when we were camping." To Gus, Nola was a shore that had the firmness of a mother, even if she was brambly. "I've never understood how people in this country take fresh water for granted."

They were escaping on Highway 53 to country where the lakes were more numerous than the towns. Still, they were momentary mirages of ore-free water past blueberry marshes, birches, and the firs that grew so tall that they had the shadowy effect of skyscrapers. Gus rambled on about the Boundary Waters, how the food chain was not being shortchanged there, how it had never suffered from dark-age septic systems.

Nola was so downcast that Gus attempted comic relief, going on about his plumbing phobia. He used to wake as if he were climbing out of a bacteria-spiked basement, its pipes like geysers in a marsh.

Then he saw that Nola was as weary as a person in a portage.

"Gus, *what* would have happened to your mind if you were a child in Duluth during the last few days? What about Sy, his body, the asbestos?"

"I feel for Sy," Gus replied. "Hopefully, it's an impurity that can be filtered out. Gees, in the purest body of freshwater."

Gus was stumbling at turn-offs, looking for a tar road. Though the desultory cabin roads weren't on the road map, Nola seized it. Its edges were like lettuce from Gus's grasp.

"Are Sy's parents having trouble getting water?" Nola asked.

"Like everybody else is. They figure that if people aren't already sick, that it's not very bad. The ages in the Duluth obits tend to be old. Gees, Minnesota of all places."

Nola was ardent for once, seeing the sign for spring water. Gus felt as if he had put his arm around her. The knotty-eyed farmer was standing near his jug-filled shed, sympathetic despite Gus's shoulder-length hair and his New York plates.

As Gus lugged gallon jugs of spring water, he saw that Nola was flipping the farmer some bills. He was chauffeur again, asking Nola if she would like something to eat down the road.

The same disdain. "I have to work tonight, Gus." But she added, "I'll make reservations for you and Sy if you want."

5

Nineteen years later in the restaurant where Nola waitressed, she is saying to Sy, "It's a city of strange catastrophes, Duluth. We seem to have this conversation whenever I see you, Sy. At least the water we're drinking is filtered now."

Richard sees that Nola isn't sorry she and Sy never got beyond this discussion about Duluth. It's something they still rib each other about, Nola's crush on Sy.

Sy is inattentive with the waitress, hearing about the recent evacuation of Duluth after a benzene spill near Lake Superior. His disgruntlement still has that stare of mutiny. But if Richard suggests anything, Sy now has a "Who, me?" attitude, what too many men have these days. Although Sy finished a graduate school program, he is tied to the telephone and computer, just treading water at work too. He seems less disappointed, but his sedentary life shows in the way the skin of his neck buckles at his shirt collar.

Sy's wife, impeccable with her make-up, looks as if she meets the edge of every schedule. She probably knows how to press and pack clothing simultaneously. Their airiness is way up there in the troposphere of the untroubled. Nola has worked in chemical rehabilitation for too long to feel gratified with people in this zone.

"My parents had friends on Park Point, near the spill," Sy said. "They got out of town early. How did you evacuate?" Now that the Lowenbrau beer and the carafe of Madeira wine are on the table, Richard can give his firsthand account of the railroad spill.

Still dazed from the last day he believed the human race was capable of getting an upper hand with its destiny, Richard begins, "We slept in that morning. After driving to Duluth with the kids the night before." Then he tells Sy about the fire department force that, despite oxygen masks, called out of megaphones from their trucks. It was a warm, holiday-blue morning. Everyone had to leave the area, they called.

"I felt like I was in a war movie," Richard says. "We flipped on the radio and learned about benzene spilling from a railroad car. Can you fathom a railroad car falling down a crumbling bank into a river? In the last month?"

Richard doesn't tell how he vacillated at the news and how he quibbled with Nola's father until Nola was afraid for their minds. Richard wanted everyone in his car. Nola's father was adamant about picking up a retired pharmacist and a deaf woman who lived near him. At the last minute, Richard wouldn't allow him to drive towards the spill alone. Nola drove her mother and the kids to the cabin of the retired pharmacist.

What Richard does tell about is the rescue mission. "Nola's father was confident that there was time to get the old people even though there were buses going around for them. According to him, we might have gotten a little bit of lung congestion. It's also hallucinogenic, the benzene gas, which is why I was concerned. I thought we could get delayed. I also wondered what kind of trip we would have."

He and Sy chuckle. Sy's wife, about to eat her prime rib, grazes her knife across it. She glances from Richard to Nola and then to the returned waitress as if she's impatient at a four-stop intersection.

Richard takes that as interest. "We were driving through the gas while the radio broadcaster was describing a blue cloud of benzene. The sky was blue and I kept asking Nola's father, Where is the blue cloud? I guess the benzene was camouflaged. Or the radio announcer was feeling its effects. We picked up the old people and think of it: more than fifty thousand people leaving town at the same time. Remember Nietzsche and that stuff about the small people and getting down to the essence of life? That's what it was. People finding themselves to be transients. I mean, we are at the mercy of the maintenance crew. And the old pharmacists were used to reading any kind of scribble. They sat there coolly looking at the sky as if they were deciphering it."

Richard pauses, waiting for Nola to dispute his version of the evacuation since he has cut a few corners. It would be reminiscent of their becoming a couple so precipitously. Especially if she started in on the hidden wish he didn't know he had, a wish to live in island isolation like his prototypes, Napoleon and Marlon Brando. She can get him into a fine truculence that might last through this dinner with Sy. Taking up his fork, Richard's hand is as shaky as one of Nola's patients.

He hasn't done what he said he would do. Other things came into his life the way Nola had. And what if she hadn't when he was student body president? What if she hadn't swiped the drugs in his dorm room after an argument? As he sat musing about the crime he couldn't report, the campus police came to search his room. The disappeared drugs were as invisible as a blue cloud on a clear day.

Conversations with Nola needed aerating lately. Richard used to say that their bond was too dire, like a drug, and that enraged Nola. More dire on her side, he hadn't said. She wanted him for everything outside of work. He was turning her down on outings, even dinner, while he was in law school. And so she wasn't upset when he decided to campaign for a political favorite, went to the office and stopped fooling around.

Richard doesn't want to talk about his bid for state legislature. It was premature. And the agency he ran afterwards, lobbying and fundraising. Not as cheerful as campaigning, the door-to-door begging, the weepy wolflike spiel about the environment, nuclear arms, planned parenthood. Tramping through small towns to their prominent homes, the "Don't want anything" door slams to their lakes, his toejambing, faces that were dull, disoriented, distrustful. Until it all became a mosaic with the shingles of an acid flashback. He practically collapsed on a rich man's doorstep.

That was when Nola remembered what Herman Hesse might have said to Nietzsche – that an intelligent man had to listen to the radio music of life. She had been looking like so many women when he realized that, besides Nola's work being excellent, her love for him was the fund. He had fouled the waters, but they were getting filtered.

Nola is still in a lackadaisical condition. Since the evacuation, her shoulders draw up at sudden sounds, the swinging doors at the restaurant's kitchen, the ringing of the telephone at the bar. Sy still has that "Who, me?" look.

"Sy, have you kept up with Gus?" Richard inquires. "Ever hear what he's doing now?"

"Lucky Gus," Sy smiles

"Which one was he?" Sy's wife wonders.

"He was the big guy. You remember, floppy hair, cheerful, dotes on everybody."

"The five-year reunion."

"Last I heard, a few years ago, he was on a research boat in the Pacific, around the latitude of Saratoga."

Nola is gazing out of the scenic windows at Lake Superior as if she's seeing something for the first time.

"Good old Gus," Richard says.

"Just think of what he sees at his spacious office," Sy says.

"Jellyfish giving him messages in the coral. Belugas asking what he's up to. Must be a good trip," Richard surmises.

"Every good boy deserves favor. Remember when he said that, when he got moody?" Sy reminds Richard.

Nola doesn't say, "And every good girl too." She just keeps gazing out at water tinted with the sunset, as if she had seen an ark go by.

THE LARGER CONCERN

Ruth's slippers were swishing on the stairs. Until now, she had called down from the top step, asking him to crunch out his cigarette.

"Randy, you've been down here all night." Waving her hand and peering through smoke. "How can you have that meeting down here?"

There were stacks of magazines and newspaper clippings in the basement now. "I can remove the greenhouse effect from this room."

Ruth was inspecting his laptop, the homepage photo of car emissions and a running analysis of air in particular cities. She pushed the back button.

"I thought you were chatting about switchgrass. Is this an anti-smoking blog?"

"It's a nut site, Ruth."

THE ONCE SMOKERS WHO KNOW THE FIGHT FOR CLEAN AIR HAS JUST BEGUN.

Ruth read, "'If attitudes and language can convert a society to be smoke-free, the same method can be applied to cars and fuel. Terms like *filthy habit* and *random killer*, infused, have proven to promote individual responsibility.' Randy, who is the Infamous Smoker?"

He had used the term Smokers Infamous at the meeting he was hosting for town addicts.

"OK, Honey. It's my blog. I've been found out anyway. Lana in the smoker's club googled it. It's just an offshoot blog that I started after visiting environmentalist sites. For ex-smokers."

"But you're not ex-smoker yet, Randy."

Upstairs, spread out on the living room floor, his daughter complained that she could smell smoke through the floorboards.

"You lie like a rug," Randy retorted.

Since Ruth took a respiratory therapy job at the Mayo Clinic, she couldn't admit to her co-workers that her husband smoked. They might think she mollified smokers or worse yet, was guaranteeing job security. Rochester wasn't a chummy town that sympathized with irrational arrangements. He and Ruth had gone out as teenagers and after they were engaged, she often told about her respiratory therapy training in the same breath that she announced how she couldn't give up Randy.

He had moped and smoked when he first went to the basement, perplexed at this agreement. After all these years, a homeowner and a sales manager at the lawn and seed company. He was used to being persecuted.

When he was engaged, nobody teased him, not since he was a toddler caught sucking his thumb.

"You had an unlucky psychology," Ruth theorized. "My smoking friends all have a sibling less than fifteen months younger than them. Their mothers were busy when they were just out of infancy."

His mother was busy with their dairy farm until most of it was converted to a sod farm. There was conflict with his little brother, a pattern that ended the day they were unloading a hefty mower from a truck. It landed on Randy's foot and he sustained multiple fractures. By the time he got his driver's license, he still had nerve damage and had to think *the pedal* instead of feeling it. Their older brother wanted the farm, Randy hated driving the mowers, and his little brother wanted to escape. He drove when Randy wanted a cigarette, cruising along the Mississippi where Randy noticed his attachment to the wheel. As soon as his little brother bought his own car, he removed himself far enough away so that he had a reason for spending hours on the road.

Randy joined the crew in town, laying sod summers, dating a beautiful girl, and then he attended college in Winona and got his B.S. He played golf as a teenager and wasn't a guy to put down. Especially since he had a mouth, ample lips, and an awry grin, a mouth people noticed less if he was smoking. When guys coolly relinquished cigarettes and joints like a girl after the weekend, he concealed his nervous need. He kept chewing his cigs, a grazing personality when most guys were going somewhere else. That only grated on him a little because he had Ruth.

Respiratory therapy was almost a passion with her. She really believed her own psychological theory, expecting that he would quit smoking once he could bury his head in her breasts thirty times a day. His smoking was between *them* until the restaurants pared smokers into a section of their own. He always remembered it as happening during the gas wars because Ruth insisted on driving up to Stillwater when they ate out.

By the time their kids were in grade school, it was schoolroom-correct to harass a smoking parent. His oldest sat as far from him as possible with his homework notebook.

"How many cigarettes a day have you smoked on an average? For how many years? I can figure out how many years you'll cut off of your life."

"In this house, we are all aware."

"Then why do you do it?"

"A worse killer is the family car. Everyday, people get into a car. Why do they do it?"

Promoted to the office, he didn't think about his smoking there. Working under Gilsmith before he retired, he handled the housing development contracts. Gilsmith made him aware of language; he had warned the company to revise their advertising. People were tired of their lawns being an assessment of their worth as a neighbor.

Probably because a woman couldn't have an ashtray near her typewriter, it was the women who first expressed their irritation at the smoke in his office. Hell, they liked the smell of burning leaves and outdoor grills. But theirs was a town that conformed. Not long after he came in, the cafeteria was sectioned into smoking and non-smoking areas, a table of women that wouldn't talk to another table of women. At the vending machines, he expressed his dislike of gasoline fumes. After the female frowns, he retaliated, frowning on mowing equipment that leaked gas and ruined lawns. The reason why people should buy their preferred brand.

"I got out my old push mower last weekend and got some exercise. It was great to smell fresh grass," he boasted.

The smokers were being sent to a smoker's break room near the equipment department. People in their town weren't terribly political; if anyone raised a banner, it would be considered rude. Campaign signs on lawns were rare and disliked. In the 1990s, the company ousted the smokers to the sidewalk at the back entryway.

"I thought this was about health," Randy said at a meeting. The other smoker in the room, a seed buyer, was scrunched in her chair after standing in below-zero weather.

The secretary stopped taking minutes. "It's like alcohol. Smokers should know they will lose something they value."

"It wastes my gas and I don't especially value that."

Gilsmith retired and Randy didn't get the promotion. He blamed it on the acrimony that polluted his office environment.

"Why don't you carpool?" he wondered when someone came in late with the excuse of car problems.

"In this town?"

"How many accidents happen here near home? At least you could set something up for bad weather."

He grabbed the chance to obtain new contracts in the Twin Cities. It had become a habit, returning from a cigarette break and elevating conversation to a larger concern.

"We need to address the problem of parched lawns in Minneapolis. It must be the city air. It's as hot everywhere else."

"It's August business, that's for sure," Fredricks, his new boss, said.

"Must be the traffic. We should do more research on the fescues that California is using."

"Grass has got to breathe, Randy. You have to, too."

Unwittingly and because he could smoke in a car, he had set himself up for anxious driving and other maniacs. His car still spurted forward while they suavely passed him. He deplored the tangle but moreso the accidents and the spring storms that slowed traffic on the freeway. When the cars were crawling, he closed the windows, afraid to smoke when cars were smoking gasoline around him, farting toxins all over people's lawns.

Having become one of the condemned, he sought out one of the few tobacco stores left in the Twin Cities, picking up magazines and on warm days, stopping at a park or a lake where he smoked on a bench, a suited dissolute.

"When are they going to forbid smoking in the parks?" he heard someone say, passing his bench.

"Randy, about the company car. The other guys are complaining about the smoke smell."

One year, his wife's application at the Mayo Clinic came through. The need for respiratory therapists had lessened at their hospital. Hadn't he noticed how many people quit smoking?

"I'd think there's an endemic of asthma. If you smoked, Ruth, you'd know that people with asthma are everywhere."

"If I stay in town, I'll be doing the ambulance and the emergency room all the time."

Lately, their dinners were on a weight-loss diet of Ruth's day, the car accident that was on the nightly news.

Everyone else could quit smoking and it was about time that Ruth used her training to help Randy. She had the patch ready and the time to talk about his stresses. His favorite ice cream was in the freezer and since he liked pistachios, bowls of them had replaced ashtrays. He had to try aromatherapy, video ballgames to keep his fingers busy, and then, it was about time that they revived their marriage with sexual pampering. Without the cigarette afterwards.

The times weren't so good, he told Ruth before she got him an extra beer. People were repairing their lawn mowers, they were learning to seed, and the sod farmers still grew grass at last year's rate. The company had to sell sod at low cost to high schools for their football fields. Contracts at housing developments had turned into paltry deals with real estate companies. That's what he was doing, convincing them to refurbish the lawns of houses up for sale.

He never could think through a tough problem without a cigarette. Sitting outside in the summer, he watched the octogenarian, Dr. Weller, drive past in his gas-guzzling Lincoln, making a hazard of himself. He felt romantic when he smoked, thinking other things could be cured.

"I was thinking about the future," he said to Fredricks. "It's about time we kept up with this ethanol thing. We should be there with switchgrass seed when the farmers are ready."

"That's good, Randy. Are you still keeping up on the research?"

"I can get a report ready."

"That's down-the-road. We'll have to sell more equipment this year. People will always garden."

"Maybe we'll have to start up those old campaigns. Terrace improvement is much cheaper than home improvement. Eradicate those disgusting weeds. The pest-free backyard."

He drove through filthy snow and then, because of the irrational bargain made during Ruth's sexual pampering, went to the basement for his smoke. His anger was normal, Ruth said, furnishing him with flex toys and worry stones.

By February, Randy was down to ten cigarettes a day and his anger had turned into fanaticism. Fredricks said that hot air was still coming out of Randy's mouth. He probably knew about his basement hobby and wondered what to do about a rabble rouser. Because Lana Waters, the online sales manager at the cheese company, had discovered his blog site, he agreed on hosting her cigarette abuse group. He had been at smoking chat rooms and brought up the subject of persecution. Suggesting persecution as a method for changing environmental habits, he was referred to an environmental site. That led to his blog and the banner he was leaving on his basement wall.

WHEN I COULD SMELL THE AIR THERE WAS SOMETHING WRONG WITH IT.

To please Ruth, he had attended a few smoking groups in Rochester. Liberals and scientific sorts liked his turn of conversation and a few had turned up at his site. People like him were interested in the success of the anti-smoking campaign. The experiment was about using the same language to see how many people disliked the present conditions of driving.

GAS IS A FILTY HABIT.
SHARE GASOLINE OR BREATHE SHARED GASOLINE.
YESTERDAY A CAR HIJACKED ITS DRIVER AND TOOK HIM TO HIS COFFIN.
DON'T START. DRIVING FOR ESCAPE COULD BE HABIT-FORMING.

At least Ruth knew about his site the night of the meeting. Lana turned up first and to help him prepare. He had aired the basement and sprayed it with freshener.

"I had no idea that your husband is an environmentalist," she said. "Has he quit smoking?"

"He's still cutting down. He's always been a difficult case. This is where he smokes, Lana. The rest of the house is smoke-free. Can you smell it?"

"We should talk about it," Lana sniffed. "That's another one! How's this? POLLUTED AIR TRAVELS WITHOUT FILL-UPS. Now I'll have to join Randy's site. He's been doing polls there."

"Polls? I'm glad he's doing something more interesting than smoking down here."

After the other five came, two quit smokers and three quitting smokers, Randy confessed where he weakened and had to have a puff.

"I thought I might go cold turkey. But the traffic jams in the Cities ruined my resolve. Does anyone like driving now?"

"Driving?" Lana said. "God, that's the worst. I yanked out my ashtray."

"I couldn't drive alone for months," said Vaughn Tribbey. His wife sang and was shrill on the subject of shared smoke.

"Didn't everyone start smoking in a car?" wondered Henry Demens, a former employee at the radio station. He now ran a video store and hadn't had a cigarette for sixty-one days.

Gwen, a young mother said, "I used to love driving. Maybe because it was a cigarette break. Now I think it's terrible and not just when the kids are in the car."

"Cars and alcohol both get along too well with cigarettes," added Mrs. Bylar, in her fifties and desirous of seeing her grandchildren grow up.

"Talking about dirty air. Cars exhale a whole cocktail of filth," Randy commented.

"Imagine inhaling it into your lungs like nicotine," Henry said.

"Driving has become a filthy habit," Randy emphasized. "I wonder how many packs of cigarette pollution a car puts into the air from here to Stillwater."

"I'd guess five cartons," said Vaughn.

"If there was another way to get around, I'd take it," Mrs. Bylar said.

"I can't stand the smell of gasoline," Randy stressed.

"You have to plug your nose against bad smells when you're quitting." Vaughn drummed his hands. "Gasoline is amongst the strongest."

"When you think of the money the government puts out to discourage smoking…"

"And the money it takes in," Henry interrupted.

"They can get tough on fuel," Randy finished.

"Raise gasoline taxes. Limit who can buy it and where they can buy it," Lana contributed.

"That's it!" Randy said. "And signs everywhere, reminding people about the air emissions and their car."

"Make those companies feel like they're on the way out," Gwen piped up. "I can't see my kids depending on fossil fuel."

"They're in the stone age," Randy agreed. "Who started the smoking guilt? What if people were made to feel personally responsible? It is…It is *so* hypocritical!" Randy buried his head in his hands, hiding his need to cough.

Ruth sent around the tray of crackers and dill dip. Then she said, "What happened to the smoking discussion? Randy, I'll get you another root beer."

Randy took a last swig but then he began coughing.

"That's right. Get that anger out," Vaughn said, getting up to whack Randy's back. "That's what musicians do."

"Down the wrong tube," Randy rasped.

"Maybe it's right to forget about smoking. Randy's involved with environmental stuff on the internet," Lana announced.

"Yeah, I'll pull up the blogs here," Randy gasped. In a town like theirs, a fanatic was dangerous unless he was accepted by a group. "Here's the latest."

Forty-three people in the last week had referred to gasoline as a filthy habit.

More than sixty people had wondered aloud if their country could ever quit its dependency on gasoline.

Thirty people had frowned on solitary drivers and attempted to set up carpools at their workplaces.

Seventy-seven people had begun a discussion about bad traffic or the latest car accident.

Fourteen people had written their congressman.

"Randy, aren't you going to the ex-smokers group this week?"

"I've gotten busy, Ruth."

She peered at his blogs.

"I don't know. This 'Guilt Them!' guy might not be someone I'd like to meet."

"I wouldn't expect every anti-smoker advocate to be upright. What about this woman? She says people should be proud of taking public transportation. It keeps people off of cigarettes." He put out his cigarette.

"Randy, I've made an appointment for you at the Mayo Clinic for your physical. It's on the fourteenth next month."

"That's only a few days before my speaking engagement. I've been invited to a meeting in the Twin Cities. It's important."

"Do you know these Green People?"

At work, people had been treating him warily and any conversation about gasoline had caused derision. He knew Fredricks was keeping an eye on his website, afraid that his employee might damage the company's reputation. His speaking engagement with an environmentalist organization had put things right. The boss patted his shoulder and said, "We're going to get a battery operated lawn mower into the display room and see how it does, Randy."

The trouble was, he couldn't write his speech without a cigarette. When he practiced it, he had to have a glass of water. There was a lump in his throat. He'd had difficulty swallowing for months.

"I'll re-schedule," Ruth said. "Is anyone from town going with you?"

"Yeah. Henry Demens is interested so far."

It was going to be a hard evening, driving to the Twin Cities with an ex-smoker. The environmentalists were probably fanatical about their smoke-free building.

Here he had re-gained his self-respect except for mornings when he coughed up mucus.

"What if it's too late?" he said and was pleased that Ruth thought he was referring to a larger concern.

WHAT A SYSTEM

Before he went wrong, Arne decided that the baby should be moved from the east room. They would have to pull down the wallpaper from the guest bedroom and his wife would probably renovate.

He was adjusting the curtains she had recently hung, kites stuck in trees all over them. The sun, pink like a stove burner, poured in. He hoped it wouldn't keep his glider grounded. Watching the islands of clouds and how their banks shifted from coral to purple, he gauged the wind. A few minutes of animation and he could see how the trees stirred. The weathervane, installed so that he could see it from this window, pointed towards the sun and hovered like his hang glider.

Slurping his coffee, he turned to watch Rae, hoping she wouldn't stir in her crib. The light made pink shadows past the bars of it. He believed she comprehended the bars in front of her. Her small world was subject to reinforcements and that frustrated her, being hamstrung.

Loping in his stockingfeet, Arne appraised the expression on her face. He wondered if she dreamed of flying.

Arne had dreamed about flying for as long as he could recall anything. It wasn't the jetting variety and he didn't flap. He sailed in the air after he took off, merely pushing off from grass with his feet. But unlike Superman, he floated. When he woke as a child, he was perplexed at his double life. It was as if his dream body, from another planet, apportioned helium. But he was shorn of flying powers in the morning and against his drowsy convictions, made to believe that his sensations had no reality. There was a cheat somewhere in this, a primal experience lost.

Why did Rae cry like every other baby on its first breathing day, he wondered. Like every other baby born, she had to be spanked into inhaling and after she was spanked, she was bound up and put behind bars. She took the sentence of infancy as sorely as other babies did. As if she remembered the remnants of another way of living. And if that enraged her, she couldn't tell anyone why.

Perhaps he remembered being conveyed in the womb, Arne had considered. But gazing outside again, he could still see the dream he still had. He flew beyond trees, able to steer himself in a supple wind that elevated into waves. He floated beyond them until all he saw was sky. He looked down but he didn't fall.

His wife, having the capacity to put his emotions in a lock-up, treated his hang gliding as a probationary privilege. Her hesitation, like the traffic lights he budged past on his way home from the lab, made his sky liberty all the more enticing. The wind didn't rule so rigidly, especially when he had learned its moods and how to ride it.

Nadine could decorate the guest bedroom however she liked, kites stuck in trees and all. Rae would forget the bars once she was walking. Arne sat in his study chair, sagging and worn from his single days. Across from his bookcase, Nadine had hung a print of a circus caravan. They visited their new novelty here, a creature clutching fuzzy solaces behind her bars, a creature they would train.

Stand-in decorations dangled above Rae like the goods of the world. From the ceiling hung the mobile of a stratosphere towards which she could only stretch her hands. A Guernsey trailed a crescent moon, geese revolved under it, cowbells sparkled like stars.

Rae protested the teasing and the torment. When the inmate she doted on, a tiger in pinstripes, bounded through the bars, when she had had enough of the unreachable, she sobbed. Nadine trammeled her into a chair where Rae was fed food that she knew was terrible. Last night, she doused a gravy of green beans over Arne's loafers.

Everything she says is getting censored. It's obvious that Rae's babbling, when she's caught talking to herself, isn't for him or Nadine. Her soliloquies are discreet, like the homesick letters Arne wrote from camp when he missed his battery-operated airplane.

He could talk rapturously about hang gliding. Nadine changed the subject; his co-workers patronized him. But when he told them about the keel jutting too high, about the glider stalling, about falling with the airspeed, he saw that they weren't going hang gliding. He was their Icarus, their insurance risk. It was as he had a carcinoma.

It wasn't for the daredevil's peril that Arne went gliding. He watched the lucky kestrel spinning on the weathervane outside. It was promising a safe take-off from the ski slope. Below, the birdfeeders joggled in a wind he could surf.

He would live out his sentence, he thought on hearing rustling in the hallway. For him, the future was full of hang gliding. Nadine had the stealth of the day's northwesterly. She swerved into the doorframe, rigged already in a house jacket that was sturdy for Rae's slops.

She threw him a sullen whisper. "Are you going?"

"The wind looks good," he said. It was like a fishing trip to him.

"Have you eaten yet?" Nadine's nightgown looks sullen too.

"I fried three eggs."

They have been lip reading. He has dismayed her because she hasn't comprehended. Her mouth is braced for turbulence as she ripples into the room and stations herself at Rae's crib.

"She probably thinks we're a couple of jailers behind those bars," he says aloud.

"Jailers?" She's resigned herself to Rae's waking up. "Are you referring to our being nurturers? How is the harness on your glider?"

He joins her at the crib, saying, "Sure as these crib bars hold." His voice is as sincere as a landing but he still makes his appeal. "It's funny we don't remember waking to bars. And how we put up with being carried where someone else wanted to go."

Rae wheezes, fumbling for her blanket.

Nadine puts her hand on his arm, pacifying him.

"Maybe you want to call and cancel. Did one of those guys pressure you into going?" Her hand is clammy. Then she rubs the layers of his clothing to see what he's wearing.

"No, I don't want to cancel. There's only three of us meeting at the slope. You wouldn't want *me* going with only one other person there. Rules, Nadine."

"You won't take off if someone doesn't show?"

"Of course not." His hand climbs along her spine to the cloud of her uncombed hair. When she first watched him hang gliding, she was like a kid hearkening after her favorite kite. During the maze of their domestic life now, she has tried to talk him into giving it up.

They watch Rae coming to, bargaining with the morning, her dawn-like cheeks billowing.

"Why is she going to cry when she opens her eyes? What else does she expect?" he whispers. "Infancy must be like a penalty. Bars and rigid controls. Other animals don't go through that. What a system."

Rae blinks and then her eyes focus. Her seriousness, looking out of sleep, frightened Arne. And then her eyes water, they hurt. She begins to weep.

Arne was thrashing along knobby ground, losing his feet. He was catching hold of the wind, being lifted into it.

"Who is she?" he wonders as Rae opens her mouth to cry.

Nadine grasps Rae and pulls her into her arms, comforting her in the way of mothers, as if she is shielding her against a tormentor.

"What is it?" she says. "Is it your work that makes you talk this way or is it marriage? You don't seem unhappy when you talk about the labs."

Rae shrieks as Nadine turns to the window. The sun is an overpowering gold face. Rae nibbles on a pacifier even though there's no nectar in it. When Arne turns, the moon sways on the mobile.

Nadine goes on talking while he gets his head clear of the cowbells in the mobile's Milky Way. "You may not believe it but babies like schedules. When you glide up over the trees and that chalet, do you feel that you're escaping a trap? Like Daedulus?"

He smiles, looking at his watch, and surveys his wife. As Nadine shakes out a diaper at the table near the window, he answers, "But what don't I do? a) I don't drink; b) I don't smoke; c) I don't go on trips without you; d) I don't want other women or men; e) I don't go into debt; f) I don't sit in front of the TV watching other people perform feats. Not any of the above. I just want to go flying for an hour or two. You can come."

"That makes me want to lock you in." Nadine is clutching a diaper pin as if it is a good luck charm.

Arne watches the weathervane outside. It's still presaging the wind he wants. He feels in his pocket for his wind meter.

"You can renovate the guest room for Rae," he says.

"That's good because I don't watch you today. You're going higher and higher." Nadine gropes for the baby overalls. "I was thinking how it would be if Rae watched me hang glide. Her mother would leave her and grow smaller and smaller. Think how horrible that would be for her."

Rae squalls, getting strapped into her overalls. Arne's arms rescue her, rocking her and then lifting her to soar as high as his head. She squeals when she can touch the Guernsey going to the moon. When she lands in her mother's arms, she's grinning.

Nadine gets her socks ready at the table. When she looks up, she sees the view outside, not Arne.

"Last time I came, you coasted so high that I couldn't see the chevrons on the sails. And then the sails merged with the cloud behind them. When you go gliding and I'm at home, I feel jags in my morning, things bucking me. I wake up nights thinking that I have to call you down out of the air."

She doesn't look at him. Her voice is as remote as high altitude. Rae dangles a foot.

"But when you went so high last time, I felt as if you wouldn't come back the same. It was as if you wanted to surpass your own species. You're too young to want that, to let go of your physical connection, to fly as if what was under you was a mouse maze. I knew you wanted to keep gliding, that you didn't care so much about the pleasure of life. It wouldn't be so elating, would it, if it just led to the darkness beyond the sky. If there was nothing underneath. Well, I suppose this is a stall, a hazard for the hang glider."

Nadine looked around, the baby still haltered in her arms. Where Arne had been is thin air.

"You're right about that," he says.

Rae's staring at the swaying mobiles, the crescent moon and the cowbells that, like stars, tilt from an intractable wind.

Acknowledgments

Grateful acknowledgment to *The WolfHead Quarterly* for publishing "Laid Off, at the Past," to *River Images* for publishing "Still Life," to *Review Americana* for publishing "Nuts and Bolts," to *Word Riot* for publishing "A Close One," and to *Prick of the Spindle* for publishing "Blizzard Ambush."

About the Author

A fiction writer and a native of Minnesota, Katherine L. Holmes holds an M.A. in Writing from the University of Minnesota. She has won The Loft's Children's Literature Prize as well as Prize Americana.